LUCK OF THE LYON

The Lyon's Den Connected World

Belle Ami

© Copyright 2023 by Belle Ami
Text by Belle Ami
Cover by Dar Albert

Dragonblade Publishing, Inc. is an imprint of Kathryn Le Veque Novels, Inc.
P.O. Box 23
Moreno Valley, CA 92556
ceo@dragonbladepublishing.com

Produced in the United States of America

First Edition November 2023
Print Edition

Reproduction of any kind except where it pertains to short quotes in relation to advertising or promotion is strictly prohibited.

All Rights Reserved.

The characters and events portrayed in this book are fictitious. Any similarity to real persons, living or dead, is purely coincidental and not intended by the author.

ARE YOU SIGNED UP FOR DRAGONBLADE'S BLOG?

You'll get the latest news and information on exclusive giveaways, exclusive excerpts, coming releases, sales, free books, cover reveals and more.

Check out our complete list of authors, too!

No spam, no junk. That's a promise!

Sign Up Here

www.dragonbladepublishing.com

Dearest Reader;

Thank you for your support of a small press. At Dragonblade Publishing, we strive to bring you the highest quality Historical Romance from some of the best authors in the business. Without your support, there is no 'us', so we sincerely hope you adore these stories and find some new favorite authors along the way.

Happy Reading!

CEO, Dragonblade Publishing

Additional Dragonblade books by Author Belle Ami

The Lost in Time Series
London Time (Book 1)
Paris Time (Book 2)
Tuscan Time (Book 3)

The Lyon's Den Series
Luck of the Lyon

Other Lyon's Den Books

Into the Lyon's Den by Jade Lee
The Scandalous Lyon by Maggi Andersen
Fed to the Lyon by Mary Lancaster
The Lyon's Lady Love by Alexa Aston
The Lyon's Laird by Hildie McQueen
The Lyon Sleeps Tonight by Elizabeth Ellen Carter
A Lyon in Her Bed by Amanda Mariel
Fall of the Lyon by Chasity Bowlin
Lyon's Prey by Anna St. Claire
Loved by the Lyon by Collette Cameron
The Lyon's Den in Winter by Whitney Blake
Kiss of the Lyon by Meara Platt
Always the Lyon Tamer by Emily E K Murdoch
To Tame the Lyon by Sky Purington
How to Steal a Lyon's Fortune by Alanna Lucas
The Lyon's Surprise by Meara Platt
A Lyon's Pride by Emily Royal
Lyon Eyes by Lynne Connolly
Tamed by the Lyon by Chasity Bowlin
Lyon Hearted by Jade Lee
The Devilish Lyon by Charlotte Wren
Lyon in the Rough by Meara Platt
Lady Luck and the Lyon by Chasity Bowlin
Rescued by the Lyon by C.H. Admirand
Pretty Little Lyon by Katherine Bone
The Courage of a Lyon by Linda Rae Sande
Pride of Lyons by Jenna Jaxon
The Lyon's Share by Cerise DeLand
The Heart of a Lyon by Anna St. Claire

Into the Lyon of Fire by Abigail Bridges
Lyon of the Highlands by Emily Royal
The Lyon's Puzzle by Sandra Sookoo
Lyon at the Altar by Lily Harlem
Captivated by the Lyon by C.H. Admirand
The Lyon's Secret by Laura Trentham
The Talons of a Lyon by Jude Knight
The Lyon and the Lamb by Elizabeth Keysian
To Claim a Lyon's Heart by Sherry Ewing
A Lyon of Her Own by Anna St. Claire
Don't Wake a Sleeping Lyon by Sara Adrien
The Lyon and the Bluestocking by E.L. Johnson
The Lyon's Perfect Mate by Cerise DeLand
The Lyon Who Loved Me by Tracy Sumner
Lyon of the Ton by Emily Royal
The Lyon's Redemption by Sandra Sookoo
Truth or Lyon by Katherine Bone

PROLOGUE

October 5, 1814
Buckinghamshire, England

THE DUCHESS OF Buckingham, Sarah Farnsworth Villiers, stood graveside on a blustery October day. A cold wind billowed her black widow's weeds around her. She drew her cloak closer and shivered. With the mayor and many of the residents of the county of Buckinghamshire here to pay their respects to a revered man, she watched the casket of her husband, Alfred Villiers, the fifth Duke of Buckingham, lowered into its final resting place. The priest concluded with the Church of England prayer.

"Amen," she answered, brushing a tear from her eye. She had known this day would come, but nothing could have prepared her for the reality and the desolation she felt. Alfred had done his best to prepare her, but her future weighed on her shoulders, as heavy as her grief.

The duke had reassured her that she would want for nothing, and her life would continue much in the same way as it had since the day they married. With time to prepare, his will and testament were ironclad, and nothing would supersede them. But who knew what manner of man the duke's nephew would be? Alfred hadn't seen hide nor hair of him since he was a boy, long before his father cut off all ties to his family.

Sarah was sure it would take some time for the solicitors to find him, which would give her much-needed time to prepare herself and get everything in order. She hoped the new duke was at least respectful and polite, and allowed her the space to continue to follow her pursuits.

The bishop in his purple robes approached Sarah and took her hand. "Your Grace, the duke will be sorely missed, but I know that you will continue his good work. I pray the dukedom's heir will be half as good a man as Alfred."

"Thank you, your excellency. We will do our best to continue my dear husband's good works and add to his legacy. And we all pray that the future duke possesses integrity and moral character and that he will follow a righteous path for the benefit of the dukedom."

The bishop nodded his approval. "Call on me, my dear, if I can be of any help to you or, of course, for any spiritual guidance." He turned to the duke's three daughters, who huddled together weeping. "My dear ladies, I grieve with you for your loss."

"Thank you, your excellency," Lady Agnes Villiers Bentwood, the duke's eldest daughter, said. "Papa would have enjoyed your sermon."

"I am glad to hear it," the bishop said.

He turned back to Sarah and smiled. "I must greet the others in attendance, but I shall call on your family as soon as I can."

"Thank you, your excellency. We shall look forward to your visit," Sarah replied.

The bishop moved along to the other members of the congregation, leaving Sarah standing with the late duke's daughters.

"I w-will m-miss him so." Elizabeth Villiers, Alfred's youngest daughter, affectionately known as Lizzie, dabbed at her eyes. "P-Papa n-never forced me into situations that m-made me nervous." She expelled a deep, shuddering breath.

Lady Agnes enfolded Lizzie in a side hug. "We'll get through this together." Sarah's heart went out to Lizzie, who had an unfortunate stutter that presented itself when she was nervous, or in this case, overcome with emotion.

Patience Villiers Arthur, the middle daughter, reached out and tucked a loose copper curl behind Lizzie's ear. "Agnes is right, dear Lizzie," she said in a tear-filled voice. "Papa lived a long and blessed life, and we must be grateful that we had him for as long as we did. I truly believe he will always be with us, won't he, Sarah?"

"I am certain of it," Sarah agreed, her own lips trembling with emotion. She had a remarkable relationship with the Villiers sisters, having known them the better part of her life. The normal animosities between stepmother and stepchildren were nonexistent. She'd married the duke nine years ago and helped plan both Agnes and Patience's weddings. She adored them, and they adored her. Their relationship was free of rivalry and jealous antics. The duke's two daughters had married well to good men and lived in London.

Agnes's husband Richard Bentwood stood steadfastly at her side. "Sarah, you and Lizzie must come stay with us in London. We'll have a jolly good time," he said. Richard was a member of Parliament and a rising star in the Whig Party, who oft had locked horns with his late father-in-law. Yet there had been a mutual admiration between them, and the duke had always treated Richard as a son, despite their political differences.

"Indeed, we shall visit the British Museum and the English Opera House, and I fancy seeing Madame Tussaud's wax figures," Patience's husband Lionel Arthur added with a warm smile. "It is said they are quite extraordinary. Also, we must see Shakespeare's *The Merchant of Venice* at The Royal Theatre, starring Edmund Kean. Everyone says it's his greatest performance." Arthur was the scion of the Sinclair family, owners of paper mills in both England and America. He wrapped his arm around Patience, who'd begun to cry again. "The English Opera House is mounting a production of Arnold's opera *Up All Night*. Alfred would have loved that."

Sarah smiled through her tears. How she adored this family, but it was Lizzie of whom Sarah was especially fond. Lizzie had been twelve years old when Sarah married the duke, barely twenty at the time. Sarah had taken Lizzie under her wing and devoted as much care and attention to her as she could.

It was not unheard of for older men in the *ton* to marry younger women, but this had been a rather extreme May-December marriage. The late duke had taken Sarah in after his best friend, Sarah's father, had committed suicide. It had not been a love match, by any means, but over time, Sarah grew to love Alfred, who treated her with respect, dignity, and kindness—something her father had never done.

She held back her tears as she regarded her family gathered by Alfred's grave. Her gaze once more wandered to Lizzie, who was so sweet and good-natured, but unbearably shy, and was only ever at ease among family and very close friends. Completely oblivious to her natural beauty, Lizzie had resigned herself to spinsterhood and divided her time between her sisters' homes and Waverly Castle, the Villiers' ancestral home.

Sarah hoped that, with time, Lizzie would be able to emerge from the security of her cocoon and become the beautiful butterfly that she was destined to be. In the meantime, Sarah was happy that Lizzie kept herself busy with her gardening.

The duke had indulged Lizzie's passion for horticulture and built her a magnificent greenhouse on the grounds of Waverly Castle, where Lizzie spent her days growing rare orchids, dwarf fruit trees, and feathery pink and white peonies that magically bloomed all year long. No one could explain why scientifically, but Sarah believed Lizzie possessed what was known as a "green thumb." Lizzie had an instinctive understanding of how to nurture plants and had filled

Waverly Castle—which wasn't really a castle, but a vast manor built in the time of the Tudors—with overflowing vases and planters brimming with beautiful flowers that bloomed all year in the greenhouse. Not to mention the luscious pineapples and other rare fruit that had become all the rage among the *ton*. It was a gift much admired by her family and those who visited the manor.

An icy wind whipped at their faces as big droplets of rain began to pelt the mourners, forcing them to make a hasty retreat. With a few brief words of condolences and farewells, the townspeople and bishop left, allowing the family a moment of privacy by the graveside.

Sarah pulled a single red rose from beneath her cape and laid it on the casket, whispering, "Sleep well, dearest." Then she nodded her thanks to the gravediggers and, knowing they were anxious to get home, handed them each a sack of coins and looped her arm through Lizzie's. "Come, let us all return to Waverly and warm ourselves before the fire. We can share our stories and memories of your dear father over tea and those delicious iced cakes that Cook has no doubt made for us. I think Alfred would have liked that very much."

Sarah would plan a more formal celebration in Alfred's honor in the spring, when warmer weather was upon them, and they could welcome the villagers as well as friends and relatives traveling from London or farther afield.

That is, if the new duke will allow it.

She would try not to dwell on her worries regarding the new duke, and what matter of man he might be. She just wanted to spend the next few days with her family, reminiscing about the late duke.

They descended the muddy slope that in summer would be as green as the emerald hills of Ireland. Here, pursuant to his wishes, the duke would rest in perpetuity overlooking the land he loved so well. Sarah hoped this new chapter in her life would bring her peace and tranquility, which was the most she could expect as a dowager duchess.

CHAPTER ONE

Whitehall, England
December 20, 1815

PHILLIP VILLIERS STARED at the tarot deck he held in his hands. He focused on his future, and what obstacles he might need to overcome to improve his lot in life. He rubbed the cards and felt a prickle of energy surge through his fingers and race up his arms. Was this the change he so desperately sought, or had he lost his mind placing his faith in a Gypsy fortune-teller named Madame La Lune? The old crone wore a burgundy cloak, and beneath the hood Phillip could see a thick mane of silvery hair and eyes that glittered black as inkblot drips on vellum.

"Shuffle the cards seven times, my lord. Then cut the deck three times and fan them out on the table," said the old soothsayer in a raspy voice. "Do not speak to me. You must allow yourself to commune with the cards and the universe. Welcome the mystical portents to make themselves known, or you will not see the truth that lies ahead."

Though he was skeptical to say the least, Phillip did as she suggested and then opened his eyes. The facedown deck of cards seemed to shimmer in the candlelight. He might not be a believer, but there was no harm in being kind to the poor old woman and allowing her to ply her trade and receive payment.

As if reading his mind, she grabbed his hands and gripped them firmly in hers. Her nails bit into his skin and her coal-black eyes bored into his. As he was startled by the speed and strength in her, his first impulse was to wrench his hands from her grasp.

"Relax, my lord," she said. "You have nothing to fear." Her meek appearance belied her powerful grip.

Had his act of kindness been a mistake? Nevertheless, he did his best to comply, taking a deep breath and letting it out slowly. From his years in the cavalry, he was always on edge, and relaxation did not come easy to him. He was a man of action, and calm contemplation was usually outside his purview.

"Choose three cards, keeping in mind what it is you seek," she bade.

It was extraordinary that his hands trembled. Phillip was a horseman, a lancer, and a pugilist, known for his daring escapades against the French. He'd recently retired from the cavalry, having been badly injured at Quatre-Bras, eleven miles south of Waterloo, while serving under Arthur Wellesley, the first Duke of Wellington. His exemplary service being recognized and rewarded had resulted in his being decorated for his bravery by His Majesty George III. When Napoleon abdicated for the second time on June 23, 1815, twenty-three years of recurrent conflict had at last come to an end.

For Phillip, regardless of the outcome, his fighting days were over. He'd lost his left eye and now wore a patch. He didn't mind the debilitation; it could have been far worse. He could have lost a limb or died as so many brave men had before him. After returning to England practically penniless but for his pension, he'd yet to find his footing. Perhaps Madame La Lune might offer up a glimpse of something regarding his future—something that could put him on the right path.

He closed his eyes and hovered his hands above the spread cards. Strangely, he began to feel a vibration in his fingers; his instinct seemed to urge him as to which cards to choose. When he opened his eyes, he had no clue what the cards were or what they might mean.

"Turn over each card, one by one," the fortune-teller told him.

In one card he discerned what looked to be a king in a chariot pulled by two black steeds. The second card displayed a naked woman surrounded by a wreath. In each of the four corners of the card was a haloed angel, a haloed eagle, a horse, and a haloed lion. At the bottom was written *Le Monde*, "the world" in French. The last card depicted what could only be Adam and Eve—a naked man and woman standing on either side of a tree whose trunk was encircled by a hissing snake with a long, forked tongue.

"Well, madam, what can you tell me about these cards?"

"Hush," she said, waving her hand as she studied the cards.

God's blood, she is a brazen old hag. He bit his tongue, wary of speaking aloud his thoughts.

"This is a powerful hand, Your Grace."

Your Grace? He almost chuckled at her form of address, but what did it matter? Anyone above her station was probably titled, in her eyes.

"All three cards are from the Major Arcana. They are indicative of the human experiences shared by all, like challenging the powers that be, falling in love, and even unexpected bad news. You are being called to consider life's lessons and how best to use them."

She pointed to the first card he'd pulled from the deck. "The first card you chose is called the World, and it represents the closing of one door and the opening of another. Your life is about to change drastically. This change of fortune is within your grasp, and it will lead to fulfillment, achievement, and completion. Great blessings await you if you embrace your destiny."

And not a moment too soon. Perhaps he would find suitable employment. But then again, who would employ a one-eyed former soldier?

The old woman tapped the next card. "The second card is the Chariot." She peered intensely into his one eye, and he held back a shudder. "There are substantial obstacles to what you seek, and you could easily take the wrong path. You must maintain focus, confidence, and determination, even though the winding path will be filled with turns and detours. Most importantly, you must understand that only through boldness can you achieve your goals."

Phillip could not help but be spellbound by the soothsayer's words. "Does the card reveal what those obstacles might be?"

The old woman shook her head. "You will know them when they present themselves, or you will not." She shrugged. "It is up to you."

What kind of answer is that? He frowned. "What about the third card?"

She tapped the third card and slid it forward. "Ah, the Lovers will be instrumental in your future."

He scoffed. "I doubt that."

"Do you have no interest in love, Your Grace?"

"Love is not what I aspire to at present."

"I see, but let me warn you, think twice before you decide what your aspirations truly are. Because if love presents itself and you resist, then it could be to your detriment."

"I am not some young swain in the first blush of youth."

"Nevertheless, each card that you have chosen here today is unique. And while they each present different challenges, they are all connected in some way. And only one key will unlock everything and reveal all."

"What is that key?"

"You."

He threw back his head and laughed. "You speak in circular riddles."

"Perhaps, but you will have to make a choice, possibly between things that are in opposition to your desire. You face a dilemma that you will have to think carefully about. You will be tested for what you truly stand for and what you truly need."

He thanked the fortune-teller and was about to pay her when she laid a hand on his arm. "Not here—let us go outside for payment."

He nodded in agreement as he glanced around and noted that the rowdy, drunken men and women had seemed to swell in numbers since his arrival. The fortune-teller followed him out of the tavern, and Phillip was about to pay her when a drunken acquaintance stumbled through the door and bade him goodnight.

"Good night to you, Helmsley." He reached into his waistcoat for his purse, turned back to the fortune-teller, and was gobsmacked. *What the devil?* The maddening woman had vanished into thin air. "How odd," he whispered to himself. Why would she leave without receiving a farthing for her services? Shaking his head and adjusting his eye patch, he decided to try his luck at the Lyon's Den. After all the cards had seemed auspicious, maybe his fortune had indeed changed.

PHILLIP RAN HIS hand over the thick green baize of the gaming table and eyed his cards. Now these were cards he could give some credence to. He made sure not to cock an eyebrow, and held his full lips still from whatever quiver might beset them. He'd be damned if he would give the earl an inkling of what cards he was holding. They'd been playing for two hours, and until now he'd barely held his own. In fact, his playing seemed uninspired, and he considered his draws rather shabby, but a quick glance at his opponent, whose gaze was fixed on his hand, told him everything there was to know.

Phillip's opponent, Lucien Radcliffe, the Earl of Dartmouth, was a friend, but that didn't matter when it came to gambling. The earl was about to lose a substantial purse—Phillip felt it in his bones. His luck was about to change, and in what better way than in a game of cards with one of the wealthiest men in England? His opponent would not suffer his loss much, aside from a bruised ego. But a win for Phillip would carry him through the days ahead and pay off his debt to the Black Widow of Whitehall, Mrs. Bessie Dove-Lyon, who owned and ran this establishment, God bless her greedy little heart of stone. Being out of the Black Widow's debt would lift his spirits immensely. He was due for a change, said the woman who'd read his fortune but a few hours ago. He felt the surge of confidence, much like when he'd ridden into battle. The Gypsy did say he must be bold, didn't she?

From the corner of his eye, he saw Bessie wandering amid the tables, greeting customers. Mostly he imagined she was evaluating the house and calculating the profits to be made. She was a fine specimen of womanhood, and everyone had heard the whispers and rumors that she was once a courtesan.

While the earl strategized, Phillip perused the elegant room, where gaming tables and red velvet-upholstered chairs were filled with London's elite and, oft times, most bored. The aristocracy was always in search of excitement and distraction. These members of the *ton* and aristocracy did not offer appeal to Phillip—rather, he saw them as an opportunity.

The center of the room was anchored by a magnificent French chandelier whose prisms of light made everything glitter and glow. The heavy red velvet drapery captured the heat from the blazing hearth and spread the warmth around the room. He glanced up and could see the ladies' gambling parlor on the second floor, where a room of Society women tried their luck betting as fiercely as the men below.

Thick-piled oriental rugs were scattered about the parquet floors, and the chairs were comfortable enough to snooze in, should Bessie's fine spirits get the better of a guest. Servants stood at the sideboard, where a delectable assortment of rich foods, many having been smuggled in from the Continent, were displayed on sterling silver platters. The rumbles in his stomach reminded him that he hadn't eaten since last night.

In a corner near the hearth, Phillip could see Admiral Snowden with a glass of port precariously balanced on his barrel belly between thick, ringed fingers. The admiral's lips flapped with his snores, much the way Phillip's horse Pegasus's lips flapped when he was feeling stress or excitement.

The earl, having glimpsed the admiral too, could not resist wagering. "I'll bet you ten guineas that glass of port will topple in the next minute."

Phillip laughed. "I'll take that wager and raise you a guinea."

"Done." It was encouraged at gaming clubs and betting establishments to bet on everything and anything. Nothing was sacred when it came to wagers, and Phillip had seen it all—bets made on whose wife would get with child first, or bets on whether it would be a boy or a girl. Even betting on life-or-death questions was fair game. Once he'd heard a wager made on whether a poor soul who collapsed was dead or alive; nothing was off-limits when it came to gambling. Addictions must be fed, and those with little or nothing to occupy their time needed distractions.

But tonight, Lady Luck was smiling on Phillip, and the proof came rather quickly. Mrs. Dove-Lyon, perceiving the inevitable stain on her carpet, gently eased the glass from the admiral's grasp and placed it on the nearby marquetry table, avoiding a catastrophe. She clapped her hands, and a woolen blanket magically appeared carried by a servant girl, which she draped over Snowden's protuberant stomach. She patted his cheek gently and, with a smile, glided away. The admiral was obviously a friend in good standing. If he chose to grab a few winks between play, his behavior would be tolerated.

Tonight, however, Admiral Snowden's slumber would not stain the carpet but line Phillip's pockets.

Bless you, my dear Mrs. Dove-Lyon. I am forever in your debt.

Bessie knew her customers well and was smart as a whip; rumor had it that she was from an illustrious family that had fallen on hard times. Her late husband, Colonel Sandstrom T. Lyon, who was much older, had built the Georgian townhouse, lavishing most of his fortune on the architecturally symmetrical brick structure, with its gabled roof and dormer windows embellished with pediments, arched tops, and ogee caps. The house was painted a distinct shade of Georgian bay blue that matched the eye color of the alluring hostess herself.

The house was charming, indeed, though when her husband suddenly died, it must have been quite a shock for Bessie to discover he'd left her penniless, with a mountain of debt and only this relic of his spendthrift ways.

Phillip had to hand it to the widow—she was cunning indeed. She'd taken a disastrous situation and turned it to her advantage. If the house was all she had, then devil beware, she would make it the most exclusive, most inviting, and most sought-after gaming establishment in all of London. She kept the riffraff at bay, provided every comfort, and kept the sharps in line. But her real coup de grâce was admitting women. Ladies were welcomed graciously and protected from the attentions of anyone who displeased them. Many of the jewels of London Society frequented the special rooms set aside for the ladies. Some of these illustrious women came costumed and masked, while others enjoyed a night on the wild side that excused them from the restrictions of polite society.

Gossip was ever prevalent amid Society, yet the ladies who frequented the Lyon's Den were protected from the wagging tongues by an unspoken dictate: *Divulge the secrets of the den and you will bear the punishment of banishment.* Although many might be tempted, they dared not risk the ostracism that would surely be their fate should they babble. Life presented few entertainments to compete with Mrs. Dove-Lyon's gambling establishment, and she protected her ladies with the fierceness of a lioness protecting her cubs.

The earl spoke his declaration, returning Phillip's attention to the card game. "Well, you won that wager, Villiers, but let's see if you can top this hand. *Séquence de quatre.* Queens." The earl's brow rose with an air of confidence. Piquet, being a French card game, used French terms, and *séquence de quatre* in this case meant a sequence of four queens. A good hand indeed.

Phillip responded with a nod, indicating he wished to carry on playing.

He glanced up again at the ladies' gaming room and spotted Lady Isabella Carrington and her ward and niece, Penelope Chambers. They sipped champagne and rolled the dice, lazily playing a game of Hazard. He'd caught sight of them on the mezzanine floor when he arrived. There was whispering among the *ton* that Penelope, a wealthy heiress, had all but ruined her chances of making a brilliant match because she'd been caught in a compromising situation with the Vicomte d'Aubert. Aubert, a rogue French aristocrat and diplomat in attendance at the king's court, had left a trail of broken hearts and tarnished reputations before decamping back to Paris.

Penelope was quite comely and had a sharp wit. Her dowry would probably be enough to attract the attention of some money-pinched toff. Phillip thought her an attractive woman, but a courtship was beyond his means. The fortune-teller's prediction came to mind, but he pushed it away. He could not pursue every young lady he happened to encounter on the off chance that she might be the one fated in the cards.

Besides, who would have him? He was the scion of a disreputable second son of a dukedom who had speculated away the family fortune in poor investments and then committed suicide. Phillip did his best not to think about his father or his cowardly act, nor did he think about the debts his father had run away from and left in his wake.

He glanced at Penelope and was disheartened to see her eyes dart away. He'd caught her outright avoiding his gaze, and it left a tightening in his chest. *One day I will come into my own, and you, Miss Chambers, will have a change of heart.*

Returning his attention to the cards, he knew the moment was ripe and his confidence returned to him. He threw down his cards, declaring *pique au cent*, "Capot!" Worth forty points, this brought his total points to one hundred and forty-one. A winning hand by any measure. Phillip felt a rush of excitement. His luck had indeed changed, and he wished he could thank the fortune-teller and pay her for her reading.

"Bravo, my friend!" The earl graciously acquiesced, clapping him on the back. "Losing to a player such as you, Villiers, is a pleasure. It was a good game. My congratulations." He waved his hand, and his footman carried over the earl's cash box, which bore his family coat of arms. He removed a velvet purse and handed it to Phillip. "This should settle things between us." He held out his hand. "If you are ever in need, call on me."

"Thank you, my lord." Phillip shook the earl's hand. Lucien was a good man, and that was a rare breed among the *ton*. They'd met at Oxford and bonded in a fight. They'd both come upon a group of toffs in their senior year plaguing a bespectacled freshman who was clearly no physical match for them.

Phillip had been walking along the path and heard the frail young man's cries for help as he was being beaten to a pulp by the four brutes, who had nothing to recommend them other than being the sons of rich and powerful members of the *ton*. A crowd of onlookers had gathered, cheering on the bullies.

Phillip took one look at the slender young man, who was curled up on the ground with his hands wrapped around his head, and knew it would be the poor fellow's last night on earth if no one stepped in to help him. At that same moment, he saw Lucien approaching from the other direction. He knew Radcliffe by name only, but in a split second their eyes met in mutual understanding, and they both nodded in agreement. Phillip and Lucien both jumped into the fray and kicked the dung out of the four bullies.

The freshman, Chester Woodstock, the son of the late Duke of Cornwall, survived his wounds, and invited Phillip and Lucien to his family's estate. He was a newly titled duke, and as such had money and means. He offered them payment, which they both declined. Then he asked them if they could teach him how to fight. And they did. With hard work and dedication, the young duke transformed himself into a muscled warrior, and the three men had remained friends ever since.

The earl rose from the table and, with a nod, turned to leave, his footman following close behind. Phillip hefted the purse in his palm, feeling as if a great weight had been lifted from his shoulders.

As if by magic, the Black Widow appeared at his side. "Congratulations, Lord Villiers. I see you are having a most lucrative night." Mrs. Dove-Lyon had addressed him with his courtesy title, being the son of a duke's brother.

The Black Widow of Whitehall had become rich because of her business acumen. The Lyon's Den was only one of many properties she owned. Phillip had his suspicions about the true nature of Bessie's business dealings. He suspected her real financial windfalls came not from the earnings of the establishment through gambling but from the matchmaking services she conducted behind the scenes. The plush, elegant room, with its crystal chandelier, sconces, and the exquisite food and French vintage wines, were all accouterments to lure her targets. Bessie was sought out by every heiress in London, and every mother of the *ton* whose daughter had acquired a tarnished reputation, to find them a titled match. A match that, without Bessie's wiles, they could never hope to land. The targets included every titled fool who stepped through the blue door of the Lyon's Den.

"Madam, it will be my great pleasure to settle things with you."

"Please join me in my office for a glass of brandy. I prefer not to conduct business amongst the guests' entertainments."

"Of course. We would not want money to sully the illusion of innocent pleasure."

Mrs. Dove-Lyon chuckled, wagging her finger at him, her blonde curls bouncing, and left him with the scent of expensive French perfume and the rustle of her silk taffeta train gliding across the floor in her wake. Behind her strode her dog and bodyguard, a burly Scotsman named Bearnard. If one wished to preserve one's masculine unmentionables, one would be wise not to incur his wrath, and by the looks of him tonight, Phillip had best proceed with caution. The man could barely conceal his snarl, and he scanned the room itching for sport as he trailed his mistress. Enjoyable sport for Bearnard was breaking bones and drawing blood.

Mrs. Dove-Lyon need only frown at someone or raise her brows in displeasure, and the unlucky chap would be dragged from the table by his collar and tossed out in the street. Not that it wasn't a fine neighborhood; it was. The Lyon's Den was in the fashionable West End, home to extravagant palaces and pristine townhomes. The gambling emporium was set back off Cleveland Row, where a footpath led to the manned and guarded blue door. If one was of the right persuasion, he would be given entry to let his hair down and partake in all manner of debauchery. The betting was fierce and competitive, the women were beautiful, and the food and drink par excellence.

Phillip relaxed, stretching his long legs out in front of him. He crossed his ankles as he puffed on a cheroot and sipped brandy from a snifter. Mrs. Dove-Lyon sat behind a French Regency desk counting out the guineas Phillip had handed her. A large leather-bound book lay open before her. Phillip imagined that hefty tome held the names of every man of worth in London, with the totaled tally of their expenditures and what was owed to the Lyon's Den.

"It is all here, Phillip. Your debt is satisfied. It seems your luck may have changed, for now." She eyed him with the experience of knowing that true compulsive gamblers never remained winners in the end, and his freedom from debt would be short-lived if he didn't curb his activities. "Have you considered marriage, Phillip?"

He shook his head and chuckled. "My intention is to remain free and unencumbered from debt and from the wiles of any woman. Besides, who would have a battle-scarred soldier like me?" Phillip pointed to the eye patch covering his missing eye. He swigged down the rest of his brandy and set the glass on the table next to him. "Thank you for the brandy, Bess. It's time I made my way to my humble abode."

"You are wrong, Phillip," she said in a firm tone. "Many a woman would be interested in a fine, strapping gentleman such as yourself. Consider my suggestion, and when the time is right for you, I will find you a bride who will provide a tidy dowry and deliver to you the life you deserve. I consider you a man of honor and integrity, a rarity among those that frequent the Lyon's Den."

Phillip, already with his hand on the doorknob, stopped and turned. "I appreciate your sentiment, Bess—let us leave it at that. Perhaps a conversation for another evening. I bid you goodnight."

Chapter Two

London, England
December 20, 1815

PHILLIP APPROACHED THE door of the rooming house that he'd temporarily called home ever since his return from Belgium. A man stepped out of the shadows, taking him by surprise, and he clenched his fists, preparing to defend himself. Phillip had to be on alert at night considering his peripheral vision had diminished since losing his left eye.

"Your Grace, Phillip Villiers, sir, may I have a moment of your time?"

What is it with this "Your Grace" business? First the fortune-teller and now this stranger.

"Do you always present yourself in the middle of the night, jumping out of dark corners? I might have brought my fists to bear on you before you proclaimed your purpose. I assume a broken nose is not what you came for. What is this about?" Phillip was tired, and the comfort of bed and hearth called to him. He had no clue what this stranger could possibly want from him. The man appeared respectable, wearing a suit, tie, and top hat, which he promptly removed respectfully and began fidgeting with.

"I'm terribly sorry, Your Grace, for catching you unawares. We have been searching for you for nearly a year, sir."

Phillip studied the man. "Who, may I ask, is *we*?"

"Why, the solicitor firm of Lewis and Woodbury, who represent your late uncle the Duke of Buckingham's estate."

"My late uncle? You mean he is deceased?" Phillip had had no contact with him since childhood, as his father and uncle had had a falling-out and never spoken again. There was also the fact that after Phillip's mother's death, his father had abandoned England and taken him to France against the duke's wishes. The duke had not even made contact after hearing of his father's death, nor had he offered to inter his father's remains at Waverly Castle, his father's ancestral home, and certainly he had not made an appearance at the funeral.

"Yes, sir, and your presence is requested so that you may hear the reading of the will and the dispensation of the estate."

Phillip's mouth gaped open. He was at a loss for words. Whyever would he need to hear the manner in which his uncle divvied up his fortune? Unless perhaps his uncle had bequeathed him some small token of his estate. *If so, my luck has certainly changed.* Perhaps the fortune-teller had been correct.

The man pulled a card from his coat pocket. "Here is Sir Gerald Lewis's card. If you would arrive promptly at nine in the morning, I will make the arrangements for Sir Gerald to receive you. We are anxious to finalize things, as this affects not just you but the duchess."

Phillip's head was spinning from everything the clerk was bombarding him with. He wasn't even aware that his uncle had remarried. He would have been in his seventies, and Phillip imagined his wife was not much younger. "Very well. I will see you tomorrow at nine." He held out his hand. "And whom do I have the pleasure of addressing?"

The man's eyes rounded behind his wire-rimmed glasses. "Why,

Will Scott, Your Grace. The pleasure is mine."

"I will let Sir Gerald know he has an exceptional man in his employ. Although he would do well not to appear out of the fog on a dreary night. A man could get himself in a lot of trouble with such careless behavior."

"Thank you, sir." Scott raised his top hat and nodded, looking a bit squeamish from the compliment. He nodded again and, without further ado, disappeared into the fog creeping ashore from the Thames River.

Phillip glanced up at the misty tendrils that encased the gas streetlights, softening the bright yellow, flickering flames. He could not help but wonder if this night could possibly hold more surprises than it already had.

Whatever his uncle had left him might not be life-changing, but it would be appreciated. And, heeding Mrs. Dove-Lyon's advice, he would not gamble it away, but rather invest it and provide for his future.

December 21, 1815
London, England

BEING OF MILITARY discipline, Phillip arrived at the black lacquered door of 8 Bowling Alley Road and checked his pocket watch: ten minutes to nine. He noted the signage on the brick building: Lewis and Woodbury, Solicitors, Westminster. He swept back the errant wavy forelock that, no matter what he did, insisted on falling onto his forehead, and opened the door.

The bell tinkled inside, announcing his entrance. Behind the reception desk was the man who'd successfully tracked him down, Will

Scott. It occurred to Phillip that Scott was perhaps a young associate and an upcoming solicitor himself. Phillip kept a low profile and acknowledged that Scott had done an admirable job of tracking him down. If the man did not succeed as a solicitor, he certainly had a future as a Bow Street Runner.

Scott pushed his glasses back up his aquiline nose, and Phillip sensed it was something he must do countless times a day, as it seemed the young man's nose did not support his glasses very well.

"Welcome, Mr. Villiers. Sir Gerald will be delighted that you are here early."

"Every man's time is precious, Mr. Scott. I might add every woman's time is also worthy of respect."

"I do most certainly agree, my lord." Phillip was glad Scott had dropped the address of *Your Grace*, which made him unbearably uncomfortable. Although *my lord* wasn't necessary either.

Scott rose from his seat. "Please make yourself comfortable and I will let Sir Gerald know you have arrived."

"Thank you!"

Phillip sat, picked up a copy of the *Times* newspaper, and read the headline:

DEATH TOLL 100,000! A DEADLY VOLCANIC ERUPTION HIT THE DUTCH EAST INDIES ISLAND OF SUMBAWA ON APRIL 5, 1815—EXPLOSION DARKENED THE SKY AND LEFT THOUSANDS DEAD. THE TSUNAMI THAT FOLLOWED KILLED THOUSANDS MORE!

Good Lord, nine months ago and this is the first we're hearing of it. It was hard to imagine what repercussions such a significant natural disaster might have. The weather had been God-awful this year and showed no signs of improving, and Phillip wondered if the volcanic eruption was to blame.

"Mr. Villiers, Sir Gerald will see you now."

Phillip lifted his tall frame from the chair and followed Scott down a hallway. He was ever conscious of his height, especially in a place of business where seating was generally made for men of a shorter stature.

Scott opened the door to an office where a portly man, who perhaps enjoyed his mutton a tad too much, sat behind an enormous carved mahogany desk. Sir Gerald's receding hairline crowned a high, intelligent forehead. Despite the lack of hair on his head, the man had well-groomed gray sideburns and a bristly mustache. He cradled in his hand a quill, his gaze fixed on the stack of papers spread across a large green blotter. Sir Gerald looked up at Phillip over his gold wire-rim glasses, appearing to size him up in a glance.

"Ah, Villiers." He laid his quill down and stood, holding out his hand. The two men shook hands, after which Sir Gerald indicated that Phillip should have a seat in one of two barrel-backed chairs before his desk. "Will!"

The younger man must have been hovering just outside the door, because he popped his head in in less than a second. "Yes, sir?"

"I will need you to witness the proceedings and take notes."

"I'm ready, sir." From behind his back Scott produced an ivory pocket notebook and a thick wooden pencil and took a seat next to Phillip.

"Very good. Lord Villiers, you should know that your uncle's will is ironclad and unalterable."

Phillip had never been addressed by any title in the cavalry, and now it seemed he was going to have to get used to it. This affair was becoming more curious with each passing moment.

"There were multiple witnesses and signatories, and he was of sound mind until the end," the solicitor continued. "There is also a stipulation. I will read the will to you without interruption, if that is agreeable to you."

Phillip nodded his assent. He had no intention of interrupting the older man, so curious was he at finding out what his uncle had stated in his last will and testament.

"After I have read the will, we will discuss the contents and transfer of assets," Sir Gerald said. After clearing his throat, he began, *"I, the Duke of Buckingham, Alfred St. James Villiers, do hereby stipulate this to be my last will and testament…"*

For the better part of thirty minutes Phillip listened, his mind reeling with every word Sir Gerald read. How was this possible? His uncle, who detested his brother, Phillip's father, had endowed Phillip with his title and left him the bulk of his estate. The duke had had three daughters with his first wife, who was now deceased. And had had no male children with his second wife—in fact, no children at all. This didn't surprise Phillip, considering his second wife must be of a similar age to the late duke. Without issue, the line of succession had led to Phillip, which apparently the duke had wholeheartedly embraced.

When Sir Gerald finished reading, he paused to take a long-needed breath and peered at Phillip over his reading glasses. "Congratulations, Your Grace. I imagine as soon as the legal filings are dispensed with, you will be anxious to travel to Waverly Castle and take possession of the dukedom."

Phillip hardly knew what to say. He was still in shock from the will, and now it seemed he would have to get used to being addressed as *Your Grace*. He felt like a fish out of water, or a man wearing someone else's clothes. "I suppose that would be the next thing for me to do." If he sounded unsure, it was because he *was* unsure.

"You have not inquired as to what stipulation the duke set forth in his addendum."

Phillip had, in truth, forgotten that there was a stipulation. Perhaps that was the missing piece that brought the whole house of cards tumbling down. "And what is the stipulation?"

Sir Gerald readjusted his spectacles and flipped through the copious pages of the will. *"Pursuant to my instructions, my nephew must accept the conditions of this addendum without reservation or complaint,"* he read. *"My duchess, Sarah Farnsworth, will continue to live at Waverly Castle as long as she desires, and because of her exacting mind and superior knowledge* of matters pertaining to the estate and all related commercial activities, my nephew, Phillip Villiers, will make no decisions without her approval as to the administration of the lands, animal husbandry, tenant farmers, the township of Buckingham, and the endowments I have left to Christ's Church, in Buckinghamshire. No decisions concerning Waverly Castle or my townhouse in London or any other properties or commercial endeavors will be made without her input and approval. I wish my nephew a long and prosperous life, and many progenies, and I am saddened that I was never able to know him better."

Sir Gerald looked up. "The addendum will require your agreement that you have accepted the terms. You must sign it before the transfer takes place."

"I'm slightly taken aback, but I have no issue or complaint regarding the addendum, nor in working with the duchess. For that matter, I have no problem with Lady Villiers living out the rest of her days at Waverly Castle."

Given that the dowager was most likely of comparable age to the duke, Phillip surmised she would be more comfortable living out her remaining years on the estate. The more he thought about it, the more he welcomed the notion of having the guidance of a wise, elderly aunt.

"It might be somewhat awkward, since I am expected to marry, and my bride and I will naturally also reside at Waverly Castle. I assume the castle is large enough to provide privacy to the dowager duchess, my future bride, and our future children. Is the duchess aware of the terms of the will?"

"The duke did apprise her of his intention, and she is aware of the duke's wishes and the stipulations put forth in his will. The duke provided well for her, and she will not be a burden or beholden to you for her day-to-day expenses."

"And she is in accordance with the notion of a future duchess taking her place?" Phillip asked. "Not in the running of the estate, of course, but in the management of the household and the social responsibilities that fall to a duchess. It might become somewhat awkward, and I would not wish to cause Her Grace any discomfort."

"The duchess has little interest in the running of households," Sir Gerald replied. "She is an unusual woman with a unique set of skills. The duke relied on her judgment in all things related to the overseeing of the tenant farmers, animal husbandry, crop production, and decisions to be made regarding the dukedom's commitments to St. Peter and St. Paul, the Anglican parish church in Buckinghamshire. The church was founded by your family two hundred years ago when James I named your ancestor George Villiers the first Duke of Buckingham."

Phillip was amazed that a duchess would concern herself with such undertakings. He was quite looking forward to meeting this masterful woman whose competence was so extraordinary. "The duchess can rest assured she will be respected and treated with the deference due her position and station."

"I will courier to the duchess that you have accepted the terms of the will and will be setting forth in a few days for Waverly Castle, as soon as you have concluded your business in London."

"Yes, that would seem reasonable." Phillip wasn't sure why, but he sensed Sir Gerald wasn't being fully transparent. It all seemed too easy to him. The fortune-teller had been so amazingly accurate in her predictions that he was inclined to wonder at the Gypsy's warnings about obstacles that lay in wait for him. The old woman's words replayed in his mind: *There are substantial obstacles to what you seek, and you could easily take the wrong course. You must maintain focus, confidence, and determination, even though the winding path will be filled with turns and detours. Most importantly, you must understand that only through boldness can you achieve your goals.*

There was no sense trying to see in the dark. He would know soon enough what those obstacles were.

CHAPTER THREE

Buckinghamshire, England
January 4, 1816

SIR GERALD HAD been wrong. It had taken Phillip a week to put his affairs in order. Part of the delay had been Sir Gerald himself, who suggested that Phillip would need suitable attire befitting his new standing and title. The solicitor arranged for an appointment with his tailor William Shudall at Burlington Gardens. Naturally, even with Sir Gerald's insistence to the venerable tailor that he should make haste, Shudall, who was King George's favorite, could not be prodded into rushing. Nor could he allow a duke to precede the king. Perish the thought.

The delay had been fine, since Phillip had not wanted to disrupt the holidays of the late duke's family and planned not to arrive at Waverly Castle until after the New Year. He spent the extra days waiting for his new clothes to be finished and meeting with Sir Gerald to pry as much information out of him about his late uncle and the dukedom that the harried solicitor could provide.

Although Phillip had asked about the duchess, Sir Gerald offered up very little about her, which Phillip found strange, given how thorough the solicitor was. Sir Gerald's words only heightened the mystery surrounding the duchess and the late duke's daughters.

"My boy, I'd rather allow your meeting to unfold and for you to form your own opinion," he had told Phillip. "It would not be circumspect of me to fill your head with preconceptions. Those kinds of things tend to come back and haunt you."

Consequently, Phillip had ridden Pegasus out of London on Friday, opting to divide the journey into two days. He spent the night at an inn in Hertfordshire and rang in the New Year at a tavern. He set off for Waverly Castle the next afternoon, having taken the opportunity to rest and allow Pegasus time to recover as well. Sir Gerald had also suggested that he take his time and allow his belongings to reach Waverly before him so that all might be prepared when he arrived.

He arrived at Waverly Castle in a drenching rain after dark, having taken a wrong turn thanks to the storm, and had not arrived at the prearranged time for dinner with the duchess. He was soaked to the bone and hungry when he made his way through the stone-pillared gate and followed the graveled drive to the beckoning lights of the Georgian manor.

Phillip squinted through rivulets of water that ran down his face at the imposing mansion that was now his, and then, God willing, would pass on to his son. His exploration of the estate would have to wait. His immediate need was a hot bath, clean clothes, and a hot meal.

He dismounted, and the groom appeared out of the gloom and introduced himself to his new employer. "Your Grace, welcome to Waverly Castle. We 'ave been much concerned, sir, as to your delay. I am George Smith, Your Grace, in charge of the stable. May I see to your steed?"

"I'm pleased to meet you, George." Phillip held out his hand, and George's eyes opened wide as he hesitantly shook his hand. Phillip imagined he was breaking some protocol, but he would never succumb to lessening anyone's worth because of some hereditary distinction. "This is Pegasus, and please see he is dried, brushed, curried, and given oats, barley, hay, and a large bucket of carrots. He is as dear to me as any person I have ever known and has been my steadfast companion through the best and worst of times." He handed the groom the reins. "I bid you good evening, George."

THE BUTLER, HENRY Stiles, tall and thin with a mane of silver hair, immaculately dressed in a formal black suit, was the textbook manifestation of a proper butler. He introduced himself, showed Phillip to his suite of rooms, and had a bath prepared for him. Henry brought in the duke's valet, Jonathan James, and suggested to Phillip that Jonathan would stay on if it was acceptable to him. The valet had proficiently seen that his trunks were unloaded, and his things were put away quickly and efficiently.

Phillip had never been coddled in his whole life. He felt like a fish out of water and wondered if he would ever get used to being a duke. He nearly cringed every time he heard Jonathan and Stiles address him as *Your Grace*.

This is going to take some getting used to.

After Phillip had bathed and shaved, Jonathan helped him into his smoking jacket. "I hope you don't mind, Your Grace, but I've taken the initiative to have your dinner served in the library."

"Thank you, Jonathan. I am famished, and it would be nice to sip a glass of brandy after dinner by the hearth. Besides, I'm interested in seeing the duke's collection of books. My years of service in the cavalry were not conducive to the pleasures of a quiet life. It will take some getting used to." Phillip cleared his throat and asked the question that had been hovering at the back of his mind since his arrival: "I suppose the duchess has retired to her rooms and it is probably late for her?"

"Yes, Your Grace, the duchess and Lady Elizabeth waited for some time for you to arrive, but after two hours had passed, they realized you must have been delayed, and they proceeded with dinner and then retired to their rooms. The duchess asked Cook to keep dinner warmed for you. If you wish, I can have Her Grace's lady's maid inquire if she is up to seeing you?"

"Oh, no, I would never disturb her privacy at this late hour. I'm sure I will see her in the morning at breakfast."

"As you wish, Your Grace."

PHILLIP STARED AT the painting above the fireplace. The woman in the portrait was the most beautiful he'd ever seen, with red hair, lily-white skin, and sapphire-blue eyes. The black velvet off-shoulder gown was a startling contrast to her skin, and her full lips glistened, giving her the appearance of having just slid her tongue over them. He imagined this was the duchess's portrait, done when she was a young woman.

What would it be like to possess a woman such as this? There was a bewitching softness in her gaze, yet her jaw was firmly set in such a way that he imagined there was nothing submissive or weak about her. She seemed every man's dream of innocence and spirit, a fetching combination. The duke had indeed been a lucky man, and Phillip now understood why he'd made such an effort to provide for her. His uncle must have been madly in love with his wife. Phillip had never given any thought to marriage, but his duty to continue the Villiers lineage and the beautiful countenance of the duchess reminded him of his duty. How he would find a woman who ignited his slumbering desire the way this woman did, he had no idea.

The crackling fire in the hearth drew his attention for a moment, and he contemplated the changes that had swept into his life. He'd gone from an uncertain future to security beyond reason in the span of a few days. Of course, he would have to develop an amicable relationship with the dowager duchess; however, he didn't imagine that would be too difficult. He'd learned from Sir Gerald that the duke had three daughters, one of whom lived at Waverly Castle. The solicitor didn't say so, but it was apparent the young woman was a spinster, and it was likely she would live out her days at Waverly. From what he could see, the manor was commodious and more than aptly designed to accommodate many occupants. He suspected he would pose no problem to the duchess and his cousin, and they would pose no concern to him.

Somewhat satisfied with his reasoning, he sipped his brandy, wondering what the future might hold. Impatient as always, he could not wait to make the acquaintance of this new family of his.

Phillip heard the door open, and he turned, expecting to see the butler. How tired was he? Apparently tired enough to hallucinate, because the woman in the painting approached him. What struck him was that the painter had not done her justice; she was even more alluring than in the portrait. Even though she wore a black, high-necked gown and bore no artifice to enhance her beauty, she was still spellbinding. Her widow's weeds couldn't conceal the curvaceously perfect proportions of her body, and nothing could dim the magnificent red hair barely contained by her coiffure. Her regal bearing and startling blue eyes held him as assuredly as if he were bound and gagged. He shook his head, trying to dispel the vision that came to him of removing the pins from her hair and seeing her tresses spread across his pillow.

He had no idea how he got to his feet, but before he could find his voice, the vision spoke to him.

"Your Grace." Her well-defined brows rose, perhaps in reaction to the look on his face. "Welcome to Waverly Castle. I am delighted to make your acquaintance." She held out her hand to shake his, and he took it, pressing lightly before her hand slipped from his. Brief as it was, a slight tremor passed between them, or maybe he'd only imagined it.

If he expected her face to suddenly grow older when she neared, he was mistaken. The glow from the fire danced across her features in warm hues of copper and gold. She was blindingly beautiful, and for some unaccountable reason, it made him angry. He couldn't help but glance at the painting, if only to confirm she was the subject.

"Dare I say that I am quite taken aback?"

"And why is that, Your Grace?"

"Well, I didn't expect… I mean, it never occurred to me that you…" His thought dangled in the air, and he couldn't find the words to finish.

She looked at her portrait, and the realization slowly reached her eyes, which glimmered with amusement. "You thought…?" Her posture strengthened, and she met his gaze. "My husband, your uncle, was much older than me."

"I should say so." He bit his tongue before he said something entirely inappropriate.

"And you are wondering why, I imagine?" The glimmer of amusement that lit her eyes deepened. She seemed to him as mysterious as the sphinx, unreadable yet beguiling. If she'd asked him to roll over like a dog, he would be loath to refuse her.

"I don't suppose it is any of my business, but I am curious, to say the least."

"Your curiosity notwithstanding, your instincts are correct. It is none of your business."

"Righto. I apologize."

She'd put him in his place, politely but assuredly.

"Apology accepted, Your Grace."

Whenever his title escaped her lips, he wanted to pound his head against a wall. He didn't feel like a duke. In fact, he felt like an imposter.

"Would it be acceptable to you if we address each other with our familiar names? I am Phillip, and it would be of comfort to me if we could dispense with the formality and perhaps become friends." *Dear Lord!* Comfort to me. *Have you no sense, man? Will she consider it brazen to suggest friendship when we have just met?*

He expected to be put in his place again. Instead, the angel before him arched her brow, and he felt an overpowering desire to trace his finger over the fineness of it. And then, as if someone had opened a window and sunshine poured through it, she smiled. "It is, of course, presumptuous, and you realize you're putting, as they say, the cart before the horse. But I accept it would be preferable, since we will be living in the same house, and it can be quite tiresome to feel you must act in a certain way when addressed." Her smile was enough to send his blood coursing through his veins and his heart pounding in his chest. "I am your aunt by marriage, Sarah Farnsworth Villiers, and I welcome you to Waverly, Your Gr—Oh, drat. It might take me a bit to overcome the habit." She inclined her head. "Phillip." Without another word, she turned to leave.

"Thank you, Sarah."

She glanced over her shoulder. "I will see you at breakfast. Lizzie is most anxious to meet you. We eat at eight, as there is always much to be done. Goodnight, Phillip."

"Goodnight, Sarah."

His thoughts were a million miles away. His imagination saw her in the black velvet gown depicted in the painting; only in the portrait in his mind, moonlight poured over her alabaster shoulders, and he held them, lowering his head in a passionate kiss.

CHAPTER FOUR

Buckinghamshire, England
January 2, 1816

SARAH RAN UP the thick royal-blue Aubusson-carpeted staircase that led to the second floor, not wanting interruption and intent on avoiding any intrusion into her thoughts. He, *Phillip*, was nothing like what she had expected. There had been so much to do after the funeral that she hadn't had much time to dwell on Sir Gerald's search for Alfred's heir. However, as the months passed, the search proved more difficult than the solicitor or she had anticipated.

Sarah knew very little about Phillip. What little she did know she'd gleaned from her husband and his solicitor—one having only known him as a boy, and the other had been circumspect in his description. She knew Phillip had been a soldier in the cavalry, served with distinction, and was severely wounded at the Battle of Waterloo. She knew he was unmarried, and she knew his age, but beyond that, she had no idea what he was like. Was he gruff, staid, or a fusspot, or, God forbid, simply boring to no end?

Meeting him had certainly defied any of her preconceived notions.

The gentleman that stood to greet her had been formidable in his stature. His penetrating gaze was engaging yet disruptive to her confidence, which she was careful not to show. A magnificent head of wavy black hair, threaded with silver, hung just below his collar. When he jumped up upon seeing her, a forelock tumbled to his forehead, and he swept it back. She suspected it happened often, as she observed his hand seemed to move as if by unconscious habit.

It frustrated her that she could not read him or gauge his demeanor. He wore a black patch over his left eye, and she shuddered at the devastation he must have felt losing his eye. But he was a seasoned warrior and had surely straddled the line between life and death many times. He knew the price of battle and the risks inherent. He displayed all the signs of military bearing and devotion to God, king, and country.

When Sarah neared him, she determined the color of his one eye and found it to be a most unusual gray that reminded her of the foamy crest of an ocean wave. She imagined that in anger, his eye would turn stormy and intimidating. In the way he looked at her, she sensed something else, a longing perhaps, and she didn't know what to make of it. He was handsome, but his features were rugged, not soft, as one usually saw in a younger man. The challenges and travails he'd faced had no doubt left their marks, imprinting deep grooves on his forehead and around his eye. Sarah imagined he was not given to smile very often, which, for no apparent reason, saddened her.

The oddest thought came to her—she wondered if he'd ever been in love—and then scolded herself. *What a preposterous thought.* If she asked herself the same question, what would her answer be? Had she loved her husband, the duke? Admittedly, not in the way of lovers. She had never felt the passion she'd read about in books. But she'd cared for him and respected him.

Love was a strange and fickle thing. Her father had loved her mother deeply and passionately and was devastated when she died giving birth to Sarah. As a child, Sarah had felt the bite of her father's coldness toward her, but had no idea why until she overheard the household staff's hushed conversation in the kitchen one day. Sarah had been devastated to find out that her father blamed her for taking away the love of his life.

Not only did he neglect Sarah, but he also began neglecting his duties to his estate, preferring to drink himself into a stupor in his study or spend his time at the gaming tables. Sarah had been forced to grow up fast, and had witnessed her father's increasingly erratic behavior. She did her best to manage the household accounts and had managed to keep things on an even keel.

One afternoon, upon returning home after visiting a friend, she discovered her father in his study, slumped over his desk, with an empty bottle of brandy beside him splattered with blood from the gaping hole in his head. The pistol that he'd used to shoot himself was still in his hand. She didn't know how she'd managed not to faint from the shock and horror of discovering her father's body, but somehow, she'd managed to stay upright and call out for help. Her father's valet Tom fetched the doctor and the local magistrate, who confirmed that the Earl of Effingham had indeed taken his own life.

Sarah soon learned that her father had invested in an importing company that never actually existed and had lost every farthing of his estate, including Sarah's dowry, on a scheme that sank faster than a rudderless ship in a hurricane.

Duke Alfred Villiers and Sarah's father, Roger Farnsworth, had been best friends at Cambridge and remained close. Sarah had no idea how Alfred received word of her father's death, but he arrived in time for the funeral and gently took command of the situation. He insisted Sarah come live with him and his daughters at Waverly Castle, but was careful to make Sarah understand that it was not pity that motivated him—it was a joy to welcome her into his family.

He did mention a letter he'd received from her father shortly before he took his life. Sarah had been stunned by the news that her father had lost everything, and she was gutted by his final rejection. He'd left no personal note to her, nothing to indicate that he was sorry or that he'd regretted his actions. And nothing that showed he loved her.

At the time, Sarah had had no choice but to accept the terms of the marriage contract. Her father's solicitor had the signed agreement, and everything had been in order. Her father had planned it weeks in advance. Not that she'd had any other prospects. With no funds, she'd never had a come-out, and with no dowry, her prospects for making a match had been nonexistent.

She didn't know what to expect if she accepted the duke's invitation—had she left one horrible situation for another? But the duke had been kind and respectful and welcomed Sarah into his home from the first day.

She had been grateful to Alfred in so many ways, even in his kindness in providing Maggie and Tom, their loyal servants, with a pension and a lovely little cottage for them to spend their remaining years.

With time, Alfred fell in love with her, and she grew to love and respect him. Her feelings for him were not romantic, but she owed him so much. Sarah convinced herself she could do far worse as a penniless girl with no dowry, and she had accepted his proposal with a few caveats that should he pass before her, she would never have to worry about the future. Alfred had been more than willing to grant her every wish.

Sarah had also worried about how the duke's daughters would react to her living at Waverly Castle. But she needn't have worried, for they were open-hearted and lovely girls who welcomed her into the family fold with warmth.

Sarah's new life gave her purpose and, eventually, a sense of contentment. Although there had been no romantic love between them, her marriage had been one of mutual respect and admiration. The hardest part had been knowing that she would grow old without having children of her own to raise and to cherish.

Sarah wiped the tears from her eyes. *Stop it! You have much to be thankful for.* And she was grateful for everything she had.

A year after Alfred's death, she still mourned his wisdom and friendship, but her life had taken on a new routine. Yes, she'd known that the day would come when the new duke would arrive to take the reins, but now that that day was finally here, Sarah did not know how to react.

She sensed the new duke to be a man of integrity, but he was an enigma to her. Even more disorienting was that she found him extremely attractive. For all she knew, the new duke had a fiancée waiting in the wings. Sarah knew firsthand that life was rarely beneficent. And while she was still young enough to marry and have children, she was certainly no debutante anticipating her come-out. Nor did she wish for the kind of all-consuming love that her father had had for her mother—a love that led to his ruin.

Closing the door of her room behind her, she strode to her writing desk and slipped her journal from a drawer. As far back as she could remember, she'd kept a record of her thoughts and feelings, and everything that had happened in her life.

As she flipped through the pages of her diary to the last entry, her eyes fell on a passage she'd written some time ago. It concerned her late father and her desire to find the identity of the man who'd swindled him:

If only I could find out who he is, then I would be able to seek justice. Surely this man has ruined more than one life, and surely he will continue to do so unless he is stopped.

Sarah expelled a deep breath as she reread the passage. Early on in their marriage, she'd asked Alfred to find the man for her, but he'd refused, saying, "My dear, do not nurture revenge in your heart. It will tear you apart and spoil every good thing that happens to you. Seeking revenge will only prolong your pain. Even if achieved, it would be a sorry victory, indeed."

"But he destroyed my life, and because of him, my father committed suicide. He was your friend, Alfred. Do you not wish to see justice served?"

"Your father paid the ultimate price for his mistakes, but ultimately, they were his mistakes to make. The swindler did not pull that trigger."

"He might as well have."

"Sarah, please leave the past in the past. Let the dead rest. It hurts me immeasurably that you may regret our marriage."

She had run to Alfred and embraced him. "Never would I regret marrying such a good man. I will try my best to forget the past; please forgive me for my ungratefulness and blindness to the pain I may have caused you."

"There is nothing to forgive." He had kissed her forehead, and they never discussed the subject again.

She always suspected that Alfred knew the identity of the man who destroyed her father, but that was a secret he took to his grave. At least her father had left a last missive to Alfred, something he had not thought to leave for her. The duke had never allowed her to read it, but he did tell her that it contained a fervent prayer that his best friend would not abandon Sarah and would care for her.

Although Alfred and she tried, Sarah never conceived. It was her biggest regret, and she often spilled tears over her disappointment. "Maybe I am barren, Alfred. I am so sorry, and will understand if you wish to divorce me."

"My dearest Sarah, nothing on this earth could persuade me to divorce you. God will provide an heir even if he isn't a result of our union. Let me never hear such words uttered from your lips again." That had been that, and their nine years together had been happy and without regret.

She picked up her quill, dipped it in the inkwell, and began to write:

> Today the new duke, Phillip Villiers, arrived and took possession of Waverly Castle. As his arrival was delayed, I only spoke to him for a few minutes and was unsure what to make of him. He is a tall, broad-shouldered man clearly used to physical activity and being out-of-doors. He wears a patch over his eye, from being injured in battle, and it gives him the look of a dashing pirate, but it does not detract from his overall appeal. The new duke has a remarkable resemblance to my late husband. Of course, a much younger version. Given his newly acquired fortune, he will surely want to marry. Providing an heir to the dukedom must indeed sit heavily on his mind, and if not yet, I'm sure it soon will. I will learn more about his manner and ways tomorrow at breakfast. I hope we can develop a friendly rapport that will benefit the dukedom. Dear Lord, who holds our lives in your hands, protect us and guide the new duke with a gentle hand to be the best he can be.

Before readying herself for bed, Sarah looked out the window. The rain had stopped, but a blustery wind blew through the trees. She thought about Phillip Villiers and her attraction to him. She made up her mind to keep their relationship strictly on a friendship basis. To step over that line could bring trouble, and she'd had enough of that to last a lifetime.

Chapter Five

Buckinghamshire, England
January 16, 1816

Sarah Farnsworth Villiers was as intelligent as she was beautiful. Phillip was grateful that she was as generous with her advice as she was with her time in showing him all the aspects of running a large estate. Because his uncle's will had been specific that she should continue her duties, it eased any tension that might have arisen between them. In fact, he'd come to rely on her sound judgment and thoughtful suggestions.

Phillip had spent every day over the past two weeks in Sarah's company, and although he'd grown quite comfortable in her presence, he hadn't dared inquire about her relationship with the late duke, nor how she'd come to be his wife. That she had been at least forty years younger than the duke was perplexing to him. He wondered what would make a beautiful, educated, and accomplished young woman decide to marry a man old enough to be her father, if not her grandfather. Yes, the duke had been wealthy beyond measure and a good man, but there were plenty of good men of means who were closer in age to her.

The lands surrounding Waverly Castle encompassed a large swath of meadow, grazing land, and planted fields well beyond what the eye could see. It belonged to the dukedom, his dukedom, and contained numerous tenant farms that raised crops and livestock. He had begun to accompany Sarah on her weekly rounds and visits with the farmers, herders, and their families. She was well liked, and they always welcomed her, inviting her in for tea. Unfortunately, tea would not bring comfort today. Phillip knew they both needed a snifter of brandy or a shot glass of Irish whiskey.

Tears streaming down her face, Sarah turned away, her hands covering her face, her shoulders shaking. "Oh, dear Lord, will I ever get used to the finality of death?" Her reaction mirrored Phillip's own. Having arrived at one of the farms, they were shown to the barn where a mare was giving birth. What should have been a happy moment of renewal of life became an agonizing ordeal that went on for hours until the distressed mare delivered a stillborn, perfectly formed colt, a lesson that death struck randomly and without reason. It was unexplainable and heart-wrenching. "She carried him for so long, and now to lose him is too cruel."

Phillip wrapped his arms around Sarah in a comforting embrace, and she buried her face in his shoulder. He said nothing rather than saying something inane, such as *life is sometimes cruel*, which a recent widow shouldn't be reminded of. Allowing her to release her pain was more important than words. Her reaction seemed so heartfelt and personal that he wondered if perhaps she and his uncle had lost a child. For some reason, he wished he could speak to her about it, could in some way offer her more than just a shoulder to cry on. A woman's tears, and Sarah's in particular, did something to him, and he would do anything to ease her comfort.

When her tears were spent, Sarah pulled away and wiped her eyes. Phillip was aware of and confused by the inescapable feeling of loss that overwhelmed him when his arms were empty of her. He tried unsuccessfully to drive the ridiculous notion from his thoughts, which were thoroughly improper. Yet the way he felt with her pressed against him had struck a chord that resonated on an unfathomable level well beyond his understanding. He chalked it up to his not having been with a woman for some time.

"Perhaps we should head back to Waverly Castle," he said. "The weather seems unpredictable, and another snowstorm looks imminent."

"Yes, of course. I apologize for losing control of my emotions. Forgive me, Phillip."

"No need." He cleared his throat to regain his own equilibrium.

The ride back was quiet, and each kept to their own counsel, not revealing their thoughts. Less than a half-mile from the house, Sarah turned to him. "I need to feel the wind in my hair and feel alive again."

He looked at her, not understanding her meaning. "And how does one go about doing this?"

Her smile was teasing, and her blue eyes held a sparkle that spoke volumes. "Why, Your Grace, I would have thought you might have guessed what I had in mind." She pulled the pins from her bun, letting them fall to the ground, and her glorious mane of red hair cascaded free. "I challenge you to a race, and I bet you a guinea I'll beat you. What say you? Are you up to abandoning your decorum and risking being beaten by a woman?"

He couldn't have been more surprised if she'd invited him to her chamber for a romp beneath the sheets, although he secretly wished she would. Instead, he met her challenge head-on. "You do know that I served in the cavalry. And in case you don't know, that marks me as a military-trained equestrian, and"—he patted Pegasus on the neck—"my friend here is a decorated war hero and as fast as the wind that you claim a desire for. Perhaps you should reconsider your wager." He grinned, rather enjoying this chameleon-like change that had come over her.

"Hmph, I never renege on a wager, but if you're not up to the challenge?" Her sidelong glance and dark fan of lashes hid her sparkling sapphire-blue orbs. Had he not known better, he could have sworn she was flirting with him. What in God's name had come over her? Had the death of the colt somehow altered her personality?

Before he could answer, she shot off like a canister from a twelve-pound cannon, making his jaw drop. She'd said she wanted to feel the wind in her hair, and, by Jiminy, it was a sight to see. He leaned over Pegasus' neck and whispered in the stallion's ear, *"Sortez-nous de là, mon ami."* *Get us out of here, my friend.* How often he had said these words to Pegasus when death had surrounded them, and their only option was escape or meet their maker. The horse had not forgotten the meaning, and neither had he.

Pegasus's hooves thundered on the ground, and in less than a second, the stallion hit his stride, and they began to gain on Sarah and her mare Lysistrata. He'd found her horse's name amusing when he first heard it. *Lysistrata*, an ancient Greek comedy by Aristophanes, argued that a man's lust for sex was far greater than his desire for war. If denied the embrace of the fairer sex forever as a condition of war, he would not live without satisfaction and would assuredly lay down his arms. He'd meant to ask her if she named the mare with that play in mind, but decorum had restrained him.

Phillip loved a challenge and would give her a run for her money, but in the end, being a gentleman, he would gift her victory. He squeezed his thighs tight and rose into a two-point position, lifting his weight from Pegasus's back. The horse answered by opening his stride, and his hooves tore at the turf.

Sarah was an excellent horsewoman, and he'd gotten over his initial shock that when riding within the dukedom's lands, she dressed in loose pants and rode *en cavalier*, astride her horse the same as a man.

Keeping a close eye on her from behind, he saw her rise into a two-point using the same strategy as he had, and nearly fell off his horse as he watched her firm, round bottom bounce temptingly before him, a mere few feet away. *Mon dieu!* Regaining his composure, he realized she would win the race fair and square, beating him at his own game.

Sarah defeated him by half a length, jumped down, and handed over the reins to the groom, who'd come running, having heard their approach. By the time Phillip was out of the saddle, she was wearing a dazzling smile and held her hand out, ready to be recompensed. The wind had swept through her hair, creating a havoc of curls, and the untamed quality of wild abandon set his heart drumming. He didn't begrudge her the guinea, and reached into his waistcoat and produced the coin before gently delivering it to her hand.

He handed Pegasus's reins to the groom. "George, please see that the horses are dried, brushed, and fed. Fill their buckets with an extra helping of carrots; they've earned them. And see they are blanketed."

"Yes, Your Grace."

By now, Phillip had gotten used to his titled address, and he nodded and followed Sarah into the house. The butler, Henry Stiles, waited in the entry, took his coat, and laid it over Sarah's riding jacket, which was draped over his arm. Sarah was busily going through the contents of a wood-painted box. The mail was kept on a handsome Georgian console table against the wall beneath a beautiful giltwood convex girandole mirror.

Phillip admired Sarah's reflection but quickly dropped his eyes, not wanting to be caught like a schoolboy gaping at his governess. She turned and held up three vellum envelopes, handing him one that was formally addressed to him.

Sarah's brows delicately came together when she spoke. "How odd that you, me, and Lizzie would receive these identical… Well, I'm not sure what they are." She turned over her envelope and examined the stamped seal of a lion.

Phillip stared at his envelope, pressing his lips closed. The return address was known to him, and he realized who the sender was. But why the Dickens would the Black Widow of Whitehall send the same missive to Sarah and Lizzie? Completely flummoxed, he silently prayed that Mrs. Dove-Lyon hadn't unwittingly, or perhaps on purpose, opened Pandora's box and delivered trouble to his door. He owed the Black Widow no gambling debt. He didn't suspect her of underhanded dealings, other than manipulating the cards in favor of the house, which wasn't the worst of sins and was known to happen at any gaming establishment. *What on God's green earth is she up to?*

"We may as well open them here together, since they appear to be the same, don't you think?" Sarah asked.

"Yes, why not?"

Sarah cracked the lion's-head seal and opened her envelope without further ado. Phillip followed suit, and inside was a sheet of delicate stationery that sparkled in the light streaming down from the half-circle fan window above the front door. The invitations were flecked with gold, and at the bottom, a seal stamped with a holly sprig hovered above the elaborately embossed initials of BDL. It was Bessie Dove-Lyon's secret seal and an invitation from the Lyon's Den's mistress. The invitation read:

Le Bal Masqué Mystère
The Mystery Masked Ball
In celebration of Mrs. Bessie Dove-Lyon's birthday.
Attendees will arrive promptly on April 1st, 1816, at the hour of seven o'clock.
Prepared to be dazzled and bewitched,
On a night you shan't soon forget.
Dinner will be served at midnight.
Expect to be home by morning light.
Admittance shall be granted
To the bearer of this golden ticket.

> *RSVP to Lyon's Gate Manor,*
> *More notably known as the Lyon's Den,*
> *Cleveland Row, Westminster, London*

"How very provocative," Sarah said with a lift of her delicate brow. "Why would this Mrs. Dove-Lyon send us invitations to such a disreputable event?"

"I have no idea." Phillip stared sheepishly at the invitation. He was sure she could read the discomfort on his face. It was best to look directly at her if he wanted to feign believable bewilderment.

Sarah rolled her bottom lip between her teeth, and his gaze settled there. It was a gesture she often did unconsciously when contemplating a matter. She apparently had no idea what effect it had on a man—well, to be blunt, what effect it had on him.

"I think…" She paused, and he could see the wheels turning in her mind. "I think this could be portentous and might be just what is needed."

"How so? You can't seriously be considering attending this event."

"Oh, but I am. I think we should do it for Lizzie."

"But you've told me countless times that it was a disaster when she attended the Season and its events, and she suffered greatly. I can't believe you would wish to force a repeat performance on her."

Sarah laid her hand on his arm, and he felt the heat of her touch through his sleeve. "This would be entirely different and empowering for her. She would be masked and costumed, allowing her to project something other than who she sees herself as. Of course, we would attend with her as proper escorts to protect her reputation. I've heard whispers of this gambling establishment and its aristocratic clientele. It might prove an opportunity for Lizzie to experience attention from the finest men in London. Who knows what might come of it?" She clapped her hands together. "Yes, I think this is exactly what is needed to bring Lizzie out of her shell."

Phillip could not imagine the change that had come over Sarah. It was as if he was in the presence of another woman. Had letting her hair loose in the wind somehow loosened her good sense? He could not fathom it. "If this is what you wish, I will oblige you. I daresay we should leave for London as soon as possible so you and Elizabeth can have new gowns made. I could use a change of pace, and I haven't yet been to our London residence. I am warming to the idea. A bit of adventure should be very stimulating." He was always careful to refer to Waverly Castle and the townhouse in London, Waverly House, as *theirs*, even though, technically, he had inherited all of the duke's properties.

"Then it is settled. I will deliver Lizzie's invitation and tell her of your decision that we all attend. I expect to receive an argument from her, but my determination is great, and she does not like to disappoint me."

Phillip could not help but smile. *Nor do I.*

CHAPTER SIX

London, England
April 1, 1816

PHILLIP ESCORTED THE ladies from the Lyon's Den to their waiting carriage, leaving the festivities of Mrs. Dove-Lyon's birthday celebration behind. Everything about the evening had soured in his mouth, except for the one time he'd broken in and managed to dance with Sarah. Holding her in his arms and spinning her around the room to the strains of a waltz had been as satisfying as winning the Derby at Epsom Downs, the highest-stakes horse race in England's Triple Crown.

One dance with her, and he felt like he was holding the world in his arms. The rest of the evening was downhill and disappointing. It was as if Sarah was the prize of the Season and every toff in London was in a mad scramble to fill her dance card. She'd been surrounded by suitors all night long. He'd spent the evening with his gaze locked on her, and ground his teeth so much that his jaw ached. The last straw had been his losing track of Lizzie, who'd wandered off and gone missing for nearly an hour. The only silver lining to the evening was that when he informed Sarah that Lizzie was missing, she'd abandoned all her beaus and joined him to search for her. Fortunately, Lizzie had returned a short time later with a rather suspect excuse of feeling dizzy and getting lost while in search of the ladies' retiring room. It sounded like complete balderdash to him; however, he held his tongue, not wanting to upset Sarah.

After Lizzie's return, Sarah insisted they remain at the ball so Lizzie might socialize and dance. Not wanting to put a damper on things, Phillip impatiently waited, hoping to escape as soon as possible. He almost kissed Lizzie when she professed a splitting headache and asked that they return home.

"I don't understand, Phillip, why you were so anxious to leave. I was having a perfectly wonderful time." Sarah removed her mask and tucked it away in her cape. "And you, Lizzie—first you disappear, and then you're suddenly overcome with a headache." She fanned herself. "The two of you, I believe, were acting in collusion."

Phillip was not about to spell out his frustrations. Especially since he wasn't quite sure where they came from or what they meant. He didn't understand his reaction to seeing Sarah surrounded by a pack of wolves, which was how he thought of her admirers. "I take exception to your painting me as a stodgy old fogey and a spoiler of fun."

Sarah turned to Lizzie. "And don't you sit quietly thinking I've forgotten you and might forget to implicate you as a traitor, Miss Green Thumb. You promised to make an effort and step out of the world you normally inhabit. Fun, Lizzie. Have you forgotten completely how to have fun? Do not let your life slip away from you; there is no reason why you shouldn't be the queen of the ball. Do not give up on finding happiness."

Lizzie stared out the window. "My dear Sarah, I promise you I haven't. I had a wonderful time tonight and a lovely conversation with Mrs. Dove-Lyon. She really is very clever and entertaining. Not at all what I expected from a woman who runs a gambling hall. She has a unique ability to get to the heart of a person. It's almost as if she can read your mind."

"I do agree," Sarah replied. "My conversation with her was most informative. She makes no secret of her intentions." She placed her hand on Phillip's sleeve. "You, my dear Phillip, hold a place in her thoughts."

Phillip felt annoyed at this bit of news. Yet the pleasure from Sarah's fingers on his arm made him bite his tongue before he expressed his consternation at being the focus of Mrs. Dove-Lyon's thoughts. *I don't give a damn what she thinks about me.* But he was not about to upset the apple cart. Instead, he politely inquired, "In what way, may I ask?"

"I believe she wants very much to help you find a bride. And I agree wholeheartedly with her. You really must marry and get on with your life. Not only is it best for your future, but it is best for the future of the dukedom. Mrs. Dove-Lyon has such a unique insight into people's characters that I am considering hiring her to find me a husband."

"What nonsense," Phillip huffed. He rubbed his temples. The conversation had taken such a turn that his head had begun to ache. *Of all things, did I just see a glimmer of a smile on Sarah's face? Has she any idea of the effect her words have on me? Blast, I am no match for her.* Before he could ask her what she found so amusing, the carriage arrived at their townhouse at Berkeley Square.

Phillip helped Lizzie and Sarah out of the carriage. Sarah sailed by him, barely pausing to say, "Nonsense to you, but not to me. I'm beginning to rethink my options, and a second marriage is a notion I must consider." She brushed past him up the steps into the grand townhouse, with its wraparound wrought-iron terraces that faced the beautiful London plane trees surrounding the elegant garden square.

God's blood, what has gotten into her? One night out, a mask, a costume, and a room full of sycophants, and the woman has developed an indomitable determination to destroy my sense of peace.

"Goodnight." Lizzie waved as she climbed the staircase. "I really must attend to this headache, and I'm ever so tired. Come, Potsy, love of my life." With a joyous bark, Potsy, Lizzie's English King Charles spaniel, scrambled up the stairs behind her.

Sarah called up to her, "And that is precisely what's wrong with you, Elizabeth Villiers. Potsy is not, should not be, and need not be the love of your life. You can do better than a dog, even if Potsy is the most perfect of beasts."

Lizzie chuckled and waved her hand dismissively. "She's on a roll, Your Grace. I leave her to you."

"Balderdash!" Sarah stamped her foot and seemed determined to have the last word. "We will continue this conversation tomorrow when you are less indisposed." Gibbons, Waverly House's butler, took Sarah's cape and Phillip's coat. "Phillip, will you join me for a cognac in the library? I am too riled up to go to my bed."

Phillip hesitated, driving the image of Sarah lying in bed with her red hair unpinned and her silky tendrils spread across a pillow. Instead, he focused on whether to call it a night or spend precious moments like this in her company. His hesitation came from not knowing which Sarah he might encounter. Would she be whimsical and mercurial or serious and analytical? She was a chameleon who often dumbfounded him and left him speechless. But even though he was in a distempered mood, he couldn't pass up the comfort of relaxing in front of a fire and exchanging conversation with her. He was aware that he'd grown impossibly fond of her, which disturbed him to the point of depriving him of sleep.

"How could I pass up such a delightful invitation?" He followed her, hoping his salutary response would take the wind out of her sails and bring out the Sarah he never seemed to get enough of.

He followed her, enjoying the view of her gown swishing back and forth in rhythm to the sway of her hips. *Dear Lord, how will I find a woman who measures up to her?*

Sarah filled two snifter glasses with amber liquid from the cut crystal decanter and handed one to him. He stretched his legs before him and said nothing, waiting for her to sit. The rustle of her gown and the crackling of wood in the hearth brought forth a sigh of contentment from Phillip.

Sarah sat opposite him and kicked off her shoes. "Forgive me, but I haven't danced in such a long time, and my feet are swollen. And I must remove this silly hat and loosen my hair." She removed the feather-plumed hat and hairpins, and her glorious red hair was set free and fell about her shoulders. She scratched her head and shook out her curls. "Ahh, such relief. Good Lord, the things we women are made to put up with."

That Sarah felt comfortable enough with him to let her hair down brought a smile to his face and a warmth to his loins. This was what marriage with the right woman must feel like—both comforting and confounding at the same time. Regardless of your station in life, when you lived with other people, the walls came tumbling down. Pretending otherwise would be foolhardy. Having spent his life devoid of the company of women for any extended period, beyond some romps amidst the sheets, he was mystified by how comfortable and pleasurable being with Sarah was. Could he possibly feel this kind of contentment with another woman? He couldn't imagine how. Yet he knew that he was expected to eventually, and it distressed him.

Sarah sipped her cognac and sighed. "I have missed London. Albert and I had some lovely times here. But I'm a country girl at heart, and managing the estate has been a saving grace for me during the upheavals in my life."

"I'm glad to hear that. I would never wish you to leave your home."

She eyed him curiously. "Thank you. However, as I said earlier, I've been considering this quite a bit. Soon you will know everything there is to know about managing the estate, and it would be wrong of me to deprive you of doing it yourself and spreading your wings. Not to mention, when you finally find her, your duchess should not have to contend with me looking over her shoulder."

"Nonsense. My uncle was clear in his wishes, and I see no reason to change anything about our established routine. Your advice is invaluable to me. And there is no duchess for me on the horizon, and I'm in no hurry to find one. Besides, we should not be talking about disruptive things that matter not." He swished the cognac in his glass and tossed it back. *Blast it. She has a way of twisting my intestines into knots. My duchess, whoever she might be, will have to accept Sarah as an integral part of my world.* "Can we please discuss another subject?"

"Yes, of course." Sarah sipped her cognac, her gaze shifting to the flames that danced in the hearth. "Do you know James Harris, the first Earl of Clarendon?"

"I've heard of him—a diplomat in His Majesty's service, if I'm not mistaken. Why do you ask?"

"He was costumed as the Sun King this evening. You might recall I danced with him."

"Yes, yes, what of him?" He couldn't hide the consternation in his voice.

"He is a widower, and we share much in common. I believe he intends to call on me."

"Does he? Why are you telling me this?" His annoyance manifested in an under-the-collar heat, forcing Phillip to loosen his ascot.

"Are you all right?"

"Ahem, yes, perfectly fine. Just got a bit warm in here."

"Really, I think the temperature is quite comfortable. Anyway, I don't want you to be surprised when Lord Clarendon visits."

Phillip refilled his glass with another two fingers of cognac and lit a cigar. He puffed agitatedly. "Consider me forewarned. What, by the way, is it that you share with this man?"

"We are both widowed and childless. He manages an estate in

Christchurch and resides at Hurn Court when he's not in London." A frown furrowed her brow, as she undoubtedly sensed his discomposure. "Really, Phillip, I would think you'd be happy to see me garner attention from such a distinguished individual."

"Frankly, I'd be happy if we were leaving for Waverly Castle tomorrow."

"Perhaps you should return early. I don't mind remaining here alone with Lizzie for a few days."

He swigged the rest of his cognac and rose. "I would never consider leaving the two of you alone without a proper escort. It's unthinkable." Before he said something he'd regret, Phillip needed to make a hasty exit. Their conversation was simmering inside him, not yet at the overflowing temperature. However, the pot would most assuredly boil over if he didn't leave soon.

"I bid you goodnight, Sarah. We can finish our discussion in the morning." He bowed and strode out the door. The last thing he wanted to do was leave her presence. But the cognac, having taken its toll, might precipitate thoughts and words that could only be misconstrued and lead to an argument. She was his dilemma, and whatever he'd learned from cavalry and military engagements was of no help to him now. He was treading on ground he'd never walked upon before. Phillip knew nothing of the transitory nature of a woman, and the emotional upswings and downswings that dictated their feelings were beyond his purview. Perhaps a good night's sleep would calm him, and Sarah might rethink her hasty decision and foolhardy words. But what if she didn't?

CHAPTER SEVEN

Buckinghamshire, England
June 1, 1816

SARAH WAS WORRIED. The weather was dreadful. In fact, it was the coldest spring in anyone's memory, and no one was prophesizing any improvement. The thought of a summer as damp and cold as the winter was enough to hang a black cloud over every man, woman, and child. Even those whose mood was always positive were being tested. But for no one was the effect of the disastrous weather more devastating than for the tenant farmers, who were fearful, and rightly so, that if the darkness and overabundance of rain continued through the summer, there would be massive crop failures and starvation in the coming year.

Granted, there was good news to celebrate. After nearly a quarter century of war with France, there was peace in England and across the Continent. The previous four years of healthy crops and solid prices had created an agricultural boom. Sarah had plowed money into new and improved farm machinery, and by rotating the crops, selective breeding, and the more productive use of arable land, the dukedom and Buckinghamshire had thrived. Last year's harvest was strong across all of Britain, but an excess of supply had kept prices low. In fact, many of the prices were less than what it cost to cultivate the harvest. On many other estates, tenant farmers unable to pay rent were abandoning their farms. A crisis was looming, and Sarah would be damned if she allowed that to happen to her farmers. She would save them at any cost. These people were her friends, and they deserved better from their landlords.

This worry had convinced Sarah to return to Waverly Castle from London early. For the moment, all thoughts of marriage had been put on hold. She wrote a hasty note to Mrs. Dove-Lyon that she had to cancel their appointment to discuss matchmaking services. Another problem was fermenting, and that was Lizzie. Since the night of Mrs. Dove-Lyon's birthday celebration, she'd become quite diffident. She avoided conversation and kept to herself more than usual, spending all her time with Potsy in the greenhouse.

Even Phillip—ever since their conversation in the library when Sarah mentioned getting married and Lord Clarendon's intention to call on her—had grown sullen and distant, speaking only when spoken to. When he looked at her, the glower on his face was most unbecoming. In truth, she missed the conviviality that had marked their relationship.

The breakfast room was so quiet that the only sound was from the scrape of cutlery against plates or the sound of chewing, sipping, and swallowing. It was dreary outside the breakfast room window, with dark clouds hovering on the horizon. Without a doubt, the short respite of cold, crisp air would end with another bout of rain. With no abatement in sight, the weather drained everyone in the household of good cheer and amiability.

Sarah could take no more. "How are things in the greenhouse, Lizzie? Has this abysmal weather affected the plants?" All this talk about the weather was as mundane as conversation could get, but

Sarah was at her wits' end.

"I should say so. There are fewer flowers and fruit, but I hope summer will eventually arrive. I don't foresee this continuing forever—at least, I hope not." Lizzie stared at her bowl of porridge and berries as if the answer might lie within. Her face displayed worry that Sarah suspected wasn't based on the weather. Sarah added to her list of things to be addressed sooner rather than later a much-needed tête-à-tête with Lizzie about what was troubling her. The girl had always confided in her; if something was wrong, Sarah needed to get to the bottom of it and help her find a solution.

"And Phillip, I would think you have some thoughts on the matter as to why we are suffering from this interminable rain and bone-chilling cold."

"I have a theory, but I have no scientific evidence." Phillip sipped his coffee and then placed the cup on its saucer.

"Please continue. I would love to hear your thoughts."

He cleared his throat. "You may have heard that a little over a year ago, Mt. Tambora erupted on an island in the Dutch East Indies. It was a deadly event that claimed thousands of lives. We only learned about the horrifying event six months after the actual occurrence. Even in as enlightened an age as we live in, news travels at a snail's pace. I believe we are feeling the repercussions of that explosion. The gases and ash spewed into the atmosphere from such a catastrophic event would be carried by the winds and would likely have an immense impact on the weather."

Sarah could see the subject of the volcanic eruption had stimulated an enthusiastic response from Phillip. His inquisitive mind was one of the things she liked best about him, and something she had lately missed. Other things attracted her as well, but she tried her best not to think about them. It would be improper. Besides, as far as she could tell, their relationship was one of friendship and nothing more.

"I did read about this volcanic eruption, but not much description was reported," she said, spreading marmalade on a slice of toast.

"My dear, as I've shared with you, I take great pleasure in studying history, particularly Greece and Rome's ancient civilizations. This eruption put me in mind of another of nature's catastrophic disasters. I have read two letters from the Roman official Pliny the Younger to the Roman historian Tacitus about the eruption of Vesuvius in 79 AD. His description is terrifying, and such an event's enormity must bear consequences for the rest of the world. I have heard that the Mt. Tambora eruption was far more powerful than Vesuvius. Hence, I fear we will suffer for some time due to this unfortunate act of nature."

Sarah folded her napkin and laid it to the left of her plate. "Well, I, for one, will not allow the rain and cold to deter me from my tasks. We do not have any control over a volcanic eruption, nor do I think we ever will. We must deal with the consequences as best we can. I planned to ride to the Willoughby farm and check on things, which is exactly what I will do. Will you join me, Phillip?"

"Yes, I will not have you traipsing around the countryside unescorted, especially with this unpredictable weather."

Sarah stood. "My dear knight in shining armor, what do you think I did before you entered my life?" She chuckled and shook her head. "Very well then. We should be off. Lizzie, you will please join us for tea upon our return."

THINGS WERE DIRE at the Willoughby farm. The harvest would indeed be meager. With Phillip's agreement, they would purchase supplemental food to tide over the Willoughbys and other tenant farmer families through tough times, and suspend rent until the following year. "Hopefully, the yield will improve by next year, and things will return to normal," Sarah said.

When the rain came, it hit with a fierceness that delayed their return to Waverly Castle. It was late afternoon before a break in the storm provided a window, and they dared ford the flooded roads and fields back to Waverly.

They were soaked and exhausted when they handed their rainwear to the butler. "Henry, His Grace and I will take tea in the library. And please tell Cook I would be most appreciative of her marvelous scones with clotted cream, as I'm famished."

"Yes, Your Grace. You should know that the Earl of Dartmouth has arrived, and he and Lady Elizabeth are in the library."

"The Earl of Dartmouth? I wonder what brings him to Buckinghamshire. Have you any idea, Phillip?"

"Not a clue, but I'm sure it's nothing serious. Lucien is enamored of Lizzie's horticulture skills and is quite taken with the flowers and fruits she grows in the greenhouse. He expressed interest in engaging her in a business arrangement. But there is one way to find out. Shall we?" Phillip motioned for Sarah to lead the way then turned back to the butler. "Henry, please see that a bedroom is prepared for the earl. It is not likely the weather will be cooperative, and he will need to stay the night."

"I will see to everything, Your Grace."

Sarah paused. "But wasn't there a tiff or a misunderstanding between the earl and Lizzie? I recall her running up the stairs and locking herself in her room when he visited last December."

"Time has a healing quality, and the earl did convey an apology to her through me."

"We will see if she has forgiven him. Lizzie has been in such a tizzy as of late. I hope she has been welcoming to the earl."

Sarah opened the doors to the library, and the earl and Lizzie, who'd been sitting on the sofa, jumped up. If Sarah was not mistaken, they had been holding hands and only broke their connection when she and Phillip entered the room. It was mystifying, but clearly Lizzie was not in a tizzy and had indeed forgiven the earl for the affront he had caused her.

Instead of saying anything, Sarah chose to let things unfold. She swept into the room and held out her hand. "Welcome to Waverly Castle, my lord. I'm sorry we weren't here to receive you. To what do we owe such an unexpected pleasure?"

Lucien kissed her hand. "I have meant to visit ever since Mrs. Dove-Lyon's birthday celebration. Especially after Phillip so graciously encouraged me to do so. You left London so abruptly that I couldn't call on you there. I apologize for not letting you know in advance of my visit. I'm afraid I behaved rather impulsively." He shared a knowing smile with a beaming Lizzie. In fact, Sarah could see Lizzie was positively glowing. Happiness filled her face, the likes of which Sarah hadn't seen in a long time.

"You, my friend, are always welcome at Waverly Castle," Phillip said, shaking hands with the earl. "I, for one, am glad for the company. If only the weather was more cooperative, we might share some outdoor sport."

The door to the library opened, and Henry wheeled a tea cart filled with all the trimmings into the room. Before taking his leave, Henry added another log to the hearth, and the warmth quickly spread throughout the room. Sarah hoped the coziness would spur a revealing conversation, because she suspected that something was afoot. She wondered how many hours Lizzie and the earl had spent together alone.

"Yes," said the earl, "if I didn't spar with my Uncle Charles weekly, I most certainly would go to seed. How about you, Phillip? What do you do to stay fit and vigorous?"

"The army taught me to exercise my body and mind, and I have continued the routine to this day. However, I sorely miss riding Pegasus and cannot wait for a sunny day to enjoy an invigorating gallop."

"I'll drink to that," Lucien agreed.

"Speaking of drinking, shall we sit and have a spot of tea? I'm sure you will agree Cook makes the best scones in all of England," Sarah said, indicating Lizzie and Lucien should resume their seats. Lizzie and the earl sat so close together it was positively titillating. Phillip and Sarah sat on the sofa across from them.

Sarah poured tea and served everyone a scone with a spoon full of jam and a generous dollop of clotted cream. They sipped silently before biting into blueberry and lemon scones, and everyone exclaimed how delicious they were. After a few minutes of sharing the latest news from London, Sarah could see the earl was withholding something and champing at the bit to share whatever it was.

"Lucien, Phillip told me he spoke to you at Mrs. Dove-Lyon's birthday celebration. I don't know why we didn't see each other."

"Yes, it is odd, but there were so many guests and such a frenzy of activity that I hope you will forgive me for not seeking you out."

"Of course, we were all so engaged with the music and the fanfare. I never asked you, Lizzie, but did you speak to Lucien at the party?"

A blush spread on Lizzie's face. "I-I... Oh bother. We may as well get this over with, Lucien."

"I'm sorry—get what over, Lizzie?" Sarah looked from her stepdaughter to Lucien.

Lucien cleared his throat and took Lizzie's hand. "I can no longer contain my joy and excitement, nor can I keep this inside. I know Lizzie feels the same about sharing our news."

"Whatever are you going on about, man?" Phillip's perplexity was written all over his face. "Please explain what the Dickens is going on. What news are you withholding?"

It would not be the last time, Sarah was sure, that she realized how daft men could be. Phillip had failed to see what was right before his eyes. "Yes, do share. I can hardly wait." A possibility had dawned on

Sarah, and she sensed the repercussions would be lasting. It seemed Lizzie's recent behavior might have an explanation after all.

"I know this will come as a great surprise to you, but I have asked Elizabeth to marry me, and she has accepted. I am the happiest and luckiest man in all of England, and we would both be grateful for your blessings."

Just about to take a sip of tea, Phillip choked and spilled the hot liquid down his shirt. "Bloody hell!" Looking contrite and realizing he'd spoken out of turn, he said, "Sorry, Sarah, I shouldn't have—"

Sarah dabbed at his shirt with a napkin. "Don't be ridiculous. You are among friends, and it was a natural reaction. There you are—Jonathan will have no trouble tidying up the stain. Please continue, Lucien."

Under Sarah's ministrations, Phillip regained his composure. "Yes, do continue, but first, I want to hear from Elizabeth. You and Lucien hardly know each other, and this is a huge step to take under the circumstances."

"It is sudden, I know, but sometimes love is like a lightning strike," Lizzie said. "Although Lucien and I got off on the wrong foot, the truth is we were smitten but didn't know it. And, unbeknownst to the other, we couldn't stop thinking about each other. When we met at the birthday party"—Lizzie looked adoringly at Lucien—"that was it. We forgot our inhibitions and allowed our attraction to take wing."

"Forgot your inhibitions? What does that mean?"

Sarah patted Phillip's hand. "Let her finish."

"When Lucien arrived today and confessed his love and proposed marriage, I said yes without any hesitation. I still can't believe..." Lizzie wiped tears from her eyes. "I thought I would never find love, never marry..." She buried her face in Lucien's shoulder.

"Shh, sweetheart, I know those are happy tears, but my heart breaks when you cry," Lucien said, his voice cracking. "If you don't cease crying this minute, I will have to kiss the tears away in front of everyone." Lizzie sniffled, and Lucien pressed a handkerchief into her hand.

"I must confess," said Sarah, "I'm completely taken aback, but I am very happy for you both." She clapped her hands enthusiastically. "Phillip, I guess we will be planning a wedding."

"I guess we will," said Phillip, obviously warming to the idea.

Lizzie wiped her eyes and looked up at Lucien, and they exchanged glances, and he nodded. She cleared her throat. "Neither Lucien nor I want a big wedding. We have decided to leave tomorrow for Gretna Green. We wish to marry immediately."

"But—"

Lizzie raised her hand, cutting Sarah off before she could protest.

"Sarah, dearest, please don't try to dissuade us. Lucien and I have discussed this thoroughly, and this is what we wish to do. Believe me, it is better this way."

"But what of your sisters? Shouldn't they be consulted?"

"Patience and Agnes will understand and realize it was a sensible decision. I am not a young maiden but a mature woman. Lucien and I will leave for the Continent for a honeymoon immediately after we are wed." Lizzie reached for Sarah's hand. "I will write to you from Florence, where we plan to go first, and apprise you of all the details. We would be delighted if you could organize a small reception for our families after our return."

"Yes, Lizzie, it will be my pleasure. I'm so happy for you, my darling." Sarah stood, Lizzie rose with her, and they embraced. "Now, I think we need to celebrate." Sarah walked to the gold bell cord and pulled it.

A minute later, the butler arrived. "Yes, Your Grace?"

"Henry, we are celebrating the good news of our dear Elizabeth and the Earl of Dartmouth's engagement. I believe a toast is in order. Would you please bring champagne?"

"My pleasure, and congratulations, Lady Elizabeth, and to you, my lord." Henry bowed.

"Thank you, Henry." Lizzie could not contain her joy and jumped up and hugged the butler, who looked stunned but pleased. It was understandable that her emotions would be heightened, as this announcement would mean an immense change in her life. Lizzie would be leaving her home, the place where she grew up. She had known the butler her whole life, and he was a pillar of her world, a man who had always been there for her as a trusted servant and protector of her and her family.

Sarah wiped a tear from her eye. She could not imagine the changes to come, but sensed a shift that would change not only Lizzie's life but her own as well. When word got out that she, a widow, and Phillip were living in the same house together without Elizabeth, the gossip would fly through the *ton* faster than a mother crow with a beak full of worms for her babies.

Had Sarah been an elderly woman, no thought would be given to the situation, but she was young. The impropriety was sure to set tongues wagging. There was nothing to be done about it but wait and see. Gossip traveled fast, and Sarah was sure it wouldn't be long before they were confronted with condemnation and whispers of an illicit affair. It didn't matter to her, but Phillip had only recently taken his place as duke, and he must command respect from the community and his peers. He needed to keep his name untarnished, or finding a respectable bride would become impossible.

Sarah felt her chest constrict with tension. Her admission to Phillip of her seeking out Mrs. Dove-Lyon had been almost said in jest. Yes, Clarendon had expressed an interest in courting her, as had other men at the ball, but Sarah hadn't really been interested at the time. She'd become quite content in her routine, spending her days working alongside Phillip and then dining with Lizzie.

But all of that was about to change, and while Sarah was thrilled for Lizzie, it did present a conundrum for her. Truth be told, she didn't really want to meet someone with an eye to marriage. But Phillip needed to marry. He needed to meet a suitable young woman and start his life properly as the duke, with a duchess by his side. Sarah glanced at Phillip as he spoke with Lucien and Lizzie and swallowed the sudden lump that had lodged in her throat. When Phillip found his future duchess, she would be happy for him, of course. So why did she feel so miserable?

It looks like Mrs. Dove-Lyon will get her wish. Not only will she need to find a husband for a dowager duchess with a potentially ruined reputation, but a duke who dared to defy convention. But, of course, a man is just a man. In contrast, a woman is always the seductress Eve, who could not resist the apple and got us all thrown out of the Garden of Eden.

Chapter Eight

Buckinghamshire, England
June 2, 1816

Sarah held Lizzie's hand as they exited the white pedimented door of Waverly Castle. "Promise me that you will write me as soon as you get to Paris."

Lizzie kissed Sarah's cheek. "Of course, my dear Sarah. And you will write to Patience and Agnes and tell them of my news?"

"Do not worry, Lizzie. I will convey your happy news to everyone and tell them we will celebrate when you return."

Phillip patted Lucien on the back as they followed the women down the stone steps. "Take good care of her, Lucien. She is a treasure."

"Lizzie is the most important person in my life. You needn't worry; I've pledged my life and heart to her. I intend to bring her joy and happiness every day for the rest of our lives. I will never let her down."

"Good man."

Waverly Castle's staff were lined up outside to say goodbye to Lizzie and wish her well. She greeted each of them, shook hands, delivered hugs, and kissed cheeks. Some of the staff were weeping, and Lizzie assured them she would visit them often. When she got to Scotty, the groundskeeper, she took his hand. "Scotty, take good care of the greenhouse. I leave it in your capable hands."

"Aye, lassie, do not be worrying about it. I will see to everything just as I always 'ave. I'll not 'ave you returning to dead flowers or trees that bear no fruit."

"Thank you, Scotty," she said, tears making her lovely eyes glitter. She took Lucien's hand and turned to offer a final smile to everyone. Potsy ran to her, whining, his canine senses alerted to something happening beyond his control. Lizzie knelt to her four-legged best friend. "Don't worry, Potsy—when I return, you will be with Lucien and me at Dartmouth House. But in the meantime, Sarah and Phillip will take such good care of you that I expect you will have gained an immense belly from all the treats, and I shall have to put you on a reducing diet."

With a last squeeze, she put Potsy down, but her emotions were obviously running high. She ran to Phillip, hugging and kissing him on his cheek, then turned to Sarah and hugged her tightly. For a long minute, the two embraced, and then, tearfully, Lizzie pulled away. She took Lucien's arm and leaned on him for support. He helped her into the carriage and followed her in, shutting the door behind him. The driver snapped the whip, and the horses trotted over the graveled, circular driveway toward the manor's gates.

Sarah waved her handkerchief at the departing carriage, and Lizzie hung out the window waving back. "I will write as soon as we reach Paris. Goodbye, Phillip. Goodbye, everyone," Lizzie called.

"Safe journey, my darling." Sarah wiped tears from her eyes.

"We will see you soon," Phillip echoed, his own voice sounding raspy to his ears.

"Are you all right, my dear?" Phillip was worried about Sarah. He knew she was ecstatic for Lizzie and her newfound happiness. Yet worry and sadness seemed to have dimmed her joy. "She will return to us, and I would trust Lucien with my life. He is a responsible and sincere man who is indeed head over heels for our Lizzie."

"It's not about Lucien and Lizzie. They will be fine. Their future is bright, and their happiness is assured. They are made of the finest gold thread, and together, they will weave a breathtaking tapestry. I will miss her desperately, though. I adore her so… But my worry is regarding something else. You see, I'm afraid our current situation is no longer tenable."

"I don't believe I understand in what way our friendship is untenable." He was careful to insert the word *friendship*, never wanting to offend her in any way, regardless of his deep feelings for her. He would rather keep his feelings to himself than admit them to her and risk losing her entirely.

"Oh, Phillip, you are so unmindful of Society's mores. How long do you think you and I can live together under the same roof without attracting the censure of Society? Believe me when I tell you this situation will not be abided, and a host of objections and condemnations will soon be upon us. I would not, selfishly, have wanted anything less for Elizabeth, but the toll will be swift and exacting for us. I must arrange a momentous change to my life and plan to move before trouble descends upon us like a thunderstorm."

"I will not hear of it," he replied. "I don't give a flying fig as to what others say. I've never moved in Society's circles, and I will certainly not begin now. Besides, you and I should not direct the course of our lives based on quidnuncs and hearsay."

"We won't have a choice, I assure you." A raindrop splashed on her cheek, and he was tempted to smooth it away with his thumb, but he didn't. The staff had already disappeared into the house, leaving Phillip and Sarah alone. But he had no right to show her physical affection.

"Come, let us go inside and play a game of draughts," Phillip said.

"I believe you beat me last time, and I would like a chance to even the score. Besides, I have a surprise for you. Given the blasted cold may persist throughout the summer, I've taken measures into my own hands and taught Henry how to make a *vin chaud*. That, my dear, is a French version of hot mulled wine, and I'm of the opinion that when it comes to food and drink, the French do it best. I promise you will forget these ridiculous notions when sitting before a blazing hearth with a steaming cup in hand, and I'm beating you in draughts." He winked at her, hoping to bring a smile to her face.

Sarah caressed his cheek and chuckled. "My dear Phillip, do you ever worry about anything?"

The softness of her hand on his cheek made his skin tingle hot, and forgetting himself, he spoke his thoughts aloud. "I worry only about your leaving Waverly Castle and my losing you forever."

Sarah's eyes widened, and she whispered, "You should not say such things. Even as loyal as they are, if the servants overhear you, it could be misconstrued and damaging to both of us."

Phillip followed Sarah into the house and whispered back, "Forgive me for speaking what is in my heart. I realize the impossibility, how unsuitable this…us…we are, but I cannot bear the thought of driving you from your home. It is I who is the interloper, not you. Can we put this aside for now, and will you join me in the library? I'm sure no harm can come to us there."

"I think we spend too much time together as it is." Sarah bent and picked up Potsy, who looked as forlorn and sad as she. Without another word, Phillip watched her go inside and climb the staircase. The rain came in a drenching cloudburst, and he hurried inside. Sarah had sensibly put him in his place, but her rejection of him caused his shoulders to slump. The day loomed large and empty before him, and doom and gloom pervaded his every thought.

You will find a way to surmount her arguments. You must.

SARAH CLIMBED THE stairs, tears pouring from her eyes. Potsy snuggled against her, his nose nestled in her neck. "You needn't worry, Potsy. Whatever I do, you will be with me. Both of us have had enough disruption for one day." She didn't understand why she was so emotionally distraught. She was truly happy for Lizzie and Lucien, and delighted that they had found love. She considered them ideally suited for each other.

So why the tears and the emptiness? She needed to distract herself and do something to take her mind off the emotional turmoil raging inside her.

She went to her room and put Potsy on his dog bed. Lizzie had transferred the bed to her this morning, and Sarah, feeling empty and without a cheerful bone in her body, covered him now with a blanket. "Be a good boy, dear heart, and I'll return soon." She left the room, climbed the back stairway to the servants' quarters, and continued to the attic.

Instead of throwing herself on her bed for a good cry, she would do something useful, something she had been meaning to do for some time. Closing the door behind her, she looked about the musty room at the neatly stacked wooden boxes that lined the wall. She lit an oil lamp and set it on an old, discarded desk that—along with other pieces of forgotten furniture, paintings, and trunks filled with clothes and toys—had been relegated to the attic. More than a century old, the belongings were stored and preserved for posterity. It was remarkable how little dust had collected, and she wondered who of the servants ever managed to find the time to sweep the floor and dust where no one was likely to notice. It reminded her of the dedication of the Villiers staff. It was remarkable how fair wages, courtesy, and kindness resulted in a harmonious relationship. How well she knew that people were more alike than not, regardless of their station or wealth.

Walking the length of the room, which spanned most of the gabled roofline of the house, she found what she was looking for. The boxes were stacked one atop the other. She had supervised their loading, and they contained a half-century of letters and papers belonging to her husband.

Sarah carried the top box over to the desk and unloaded the contents into neat piles, and then, knowing this might take some time, she pulled over a Queen Anne chair that had once been part of a set of dining chairs. With a saint's patience, she opened the envelopes and began to read.

The first box contained correspondence with friends and family, invitations, and legal documents, most of a recent nature. It wasn't until she got to the third box that she found accounting ledgers pertaining to the dukedom that preceded her arrival at Waverly Castle. It was curiosity that made her open the ledger that corresponded to the time of her arrival. *Ten years ago.* Where had the time gone?

A flood of memories overwhelmed her, and she blinked back the tears. She'd arrived at Waverly Castle barely eighteen and still in shock from the horrible event that had left her destitute and an orphan. Shy and ashamed of what her father had done, she was reticent and only answered when spoken to. She tried to make herself invisible and fit in as best as she could. She'd expected to be treated like a servant, or like one of those women she'd read about in novels—women who were forced to became governesses or companions to earn their keep. So few possibilities were open to women, even in the civilized world of modern England. These indigent women were often handed off to friends or family who took pity on them and brought them into their homes. Still, this kindness was many times a mask for an underlying resentment. Their charity was rarely given without a constant reminder of the direness of the recipient's circumstances and the generosity of the beneficence to these poor souls.

In her case, how wrong she had been. It took a short time for Alfred and the Villiers girls to break down the self-imposed barriers and preconceptions she'd erected. He and the girls made her feel loved and a part of their family, and no one ever looked back. She became a sister to the girls, and to Alfred she became a confidante. He was lonely, and she was enamored of growing things and animals and enjoyed accompanying him as he managed the estate.

At first, she acted as a sounding board and secretary, taking notes for him. However, in short order, he discovered she had a head for numbers. Over the next two years, he trained her in all things regarding the estate and its management, and, in the process, Alfred grew to love her and Sarah grew to love him. Their marriage was inevitable and more than satisfactory. Her barrenness had been heartbreaking, but it marked the only disappointment in an otherwise respectful and loving union.

Lost in remembrance as she flipped the pages of the ledger, she almost didn't notice the envelope stuck in the back pocket amid a group of old invoices. She turned the envelope over and gasped in shock. It fell from her fingers, and she clutched the chair arms to steady herself. Sarah recognized her father's cursive and what he called his small rebellion of writing his Fs backward. Her heart pumped like she were a knight about to collide with another in a jousting match. It took several seconds to regain her equilibrium. Taking a deep breath, she picked up the envelope and, with trembling fingers, extracted the letter and began to read:

June 10, 1806

My dearest friend,

By the time you receive this letter, I will have taken the coward's way out. Who would ever have imagined that the young man with such grand aspirations at Cambridge would end his life ignominiously? If I am lucky and don't go straight to hell, perhaps God will grant my wish, and I will be allowed to join my darling Madeline for eternity. But before I make that journey, whether to heaven or hell, I have a request to make of you, my stalwart friend.

I have failed in the one task she left to me. To provide, love, and care for our daughter Sarah. She will never know how great my regrets are. To ask for her forgiveness would be presumptuous and misguided. It is better she hates me, for it will make her stronger. Hatred is a powerful emotion; trust me, I know.

I should have come to you for advice and help, which I know you would have offered and given. But it is wrong for you to be made responsible for what George did; you are not your brother's keeper, and no brothers could have been more different in character than you and George. Desperate to save our good name, I invested everything I had left in George's foolish scheme, only to lose it all. I cannot face the future of losing our home and the estate that has been in our family for generations. I cannot face my Sarah living in destitution; she deserves so much more.

I pray that you, Alfred, my dearest friend, will take my darling girl into your home and care for her in honor of our friendship and the love you bore Madeline. It is all my fault that my dear daughter has no dowry, not even her mother's jewelry, nothing more than the clothes she will arrive with, but she is as intelligent as any man and good-natured as any woman alive. I give to you my most precious possession, my daughter. Please do not let Society destroy her. Sarah is all that is good and kind in this world. She is the spitting image of my dear, departed wife, both in mind and spirit. I wish I could have been a good father to her, but I have failed her. I hope that one day she can forgive me.

Please find it in your heart to do well by her. There is no more to say except that I am sorry.

Pray for me.

I hope that one day, we shall meet again, my friend. If not, farewell, and know that you were the best friend that I ever had.

Roger

Sarah could barely read her father's signature through the tears that blurred her eyes. The man who'd caused her father's death was Alfred's brother George. But what tore her heart into shreds was that George was Phillip's father. Did Phillip know what his father had done? And if so, why hadn't he told her?

She was reminded of the old German proverb: *The apple does not fall far from the tree.* It was hard to imagine Phillip as being devious and conniving as his father had been…but could it be possible? *How could Phillip not know that his own father brought about the ruination of my family?*

Sarah gave in to her sorrow, so great was her pain. It felt as great as the day she'd discovered her father's body in his study. Perhaps even more so, because she now knew that he'd regretted how he treated her, regretted that he'd shut her out of his life. "Oh, why didn't you just talk to me, Father?" she cried out, as though he could hear her.

Sarah wiped her tear-filled eyes and put everything back in the box except for the letter, which she stashed in her pocket. She knew what she must do, and she must do it soon.

Chapter Nine

Buckinghamshire, England
June 3, 1816

PHILLIP HAD HARDLY slept a wink and only fell into a deep sleep in the early-morning hours. When he did wake, the sun was high in the sky, and the day was well underway. *Blast it! I've missed breakfast with Sarah by now.*

A few minutes later, he entered the breakfast room. His breakfast of porridge, eggs, bacon, and kippers was on the buffet, kept warm in chafing dishes, but there was no sign of Sarah. He pulled the cord that summoned Henry and waited mere seconds for him to appear.

"Good morning, Henry. I suppose the duchess has finished breakfast and returned to her rooms to prepare for the day? Would you please send word to her that I would like her to join me whilst I have breakfast, as I have things to discuss with her?"

Henry seemed to hesitate, and Phillip sensed the unease and tension in the usually even-tempered butler. Something was wrong. Something was very wrong.

"Henry, tell me what has happened."

The butler cleared his throat. "Your Grace, the duchess left for London just after dawn. She and her lady's maid packed up what would be needed for an extended stay."

"I beg your pardon?"

"The duchess left for Waverly House with Sally this morning. She said she would stay in London at least until the end of the Season in late June. Did you not see the letter she left for you, Your Grace?"

"What letter?" Phillip's growing anger and worry reduced his ability to respond diplomatically. He'd reverted to his military training. His terse questions and tone had the butler gaping at him with wide eyes.

Phillip took a deep breath and expelled it slowly. It was not Henry's fault that Sarah had behaved in such a rash manner. But it *was* Henry's fault that he didn't wake Phillip and tell him before she was already halfway to London.

The butler pointed to the envelope peeking out from beneath Phillip's place setting. "There, Your Grace. The duchess placed it there herself."

Phillip's face warmed; he hadn't noticed the letter, and slid it out, recognizing Sarah's elegant handwriting immediately. "I'm sorry, Henry. Please forgive my shortness with you. I had no idea the duchess was leaving, and now… Well, I have no idea what I will do about it."

"Let me know, Your Grace, if there is anything I can do to help."

"Thank you."

Phillip waited until Henry had excused himself, and then he opened the letter and began to read:

My dear Phillip:

Forgive me for leaving without discussing my plans with you ahead of time. But we both know it would have only led to an argument—you expressing your adamance and determination to convince me that remaining at Waverly Castle is right for me. And me desperately trying to hold on to whatever good name I still command. I will not become a focus of gossipmongers, nor will I disgrace the Villiers name. The very least that I owe Alfred is not to sully his family's reputation. I can't think of what he was thinking when he concocted this ridiculous situation.

It may have been proper when Lizzie was living here, but now that she is married and has left on her honeymoon, I can no longer remain at Waverly Castle.

I have made up my mind and will not be dissuaded. I must see to my future, so that you will be able to see to yours. That is why I fled like a thief in the night. I do not wish to engage in an argument with you. You can be ever so bullheaded that I find it nearly impossible to hold on to my pride when faced with your resolve and earnest persuasion.

I will stay at Waverly House for as long as you will allow, but if you wish me to leave, I will search for other accommodations. Certainly, Patience or Agnes would welcome me until I find a suitable townhouse nearby.

I wish you a wonderful life, and I know you are ready to take on the responsibilities of the Buckingham estate. Now that I am gone, I hope you will be encouraged to seek your own happiness, find your duchess, and ensure the succession of the Villiers dukedom.

My affection for you will always remain.

Your friend,
Sarah Farnsworth Villiers
Dowager Duchess of the Dukedom of Buckingham

Phillip's first instinct was to tear the letter into little bits, and only a deep breath and exhale, combined with exerting the most extraordinary self-control over his simmering anger, stopped him from doing just that. The letter left him furious—it insulted his dignity that Sarah would ever think he would turn her out from Waverly House and send her packing. The woman did more than just exasperate him; she was the only person capable of stealing whatever peace of mind he'd ever known.

Sarah, Sarah, Sarah, why are you doing this to me... To us?

Forget that she closed the letter with "your friend." That irked him beyond measure.

But Phillip knew he could not possibly be happy until he found a way to bring Sarah home. In his mind, he knew it was selfish, but he didn't care. He had never chosen the easy path and would not choose it now. Even as he assured himself that she would suffer from her rashness, he knew he would suffer far more. He would be relegated to the countryside, where he knew no one. He would be left to count the hours and days that ticked away without her. Even the weather was conspiring against him. Where he might have taken some comfort in riding Pegasus, a swim in the lake, or even an early-morning hunt, these too he would be deprived of due to the inclement weather.

Whatever happiness and security Phillip had derived from becoming a duke meant nothing without Sarah. She had become so integral to his life that the thought of a day without her was unbearable.

SARAH AND SALLY were exhausted, as were the horses. Tom, the coachman, suggested there was a comfortable inn in High Wycombe where they might find accommodation for the night. With the horses rested, they could leave in the morning and arrive in London before afternoon tea.

High Wycombe was an industrial town noted for its corn mills, sawmills, and paper mills, and was situated on the magnificent Wye River that stretched from the mountains of mid-Wales and flowed south, rambling through green hills, open meadows, and dense forests.

After settling into her room and changing her traveling clothes, Sarah left Sally and went downstairs to the tavern for refreshment.

The tavern was empty when Sarah sat down. She ordered tea and was spreading jam on a blueberry corn scone that was a lauded favorite in High Wycombe when a woman approached her table. Sarah hadn't seen the woman come in and was taken aback when she seemed to appear out of nowhere.

"Dearie, would you mind if I rest for a wee bit at yer table? I've come a long way and my bones are weary. A pleasant conversation with a lovely lady such as yerself would be much appreciated."

The woman wore a purple mantle that covered her from head to toe, and strands of silver hair caught the light when she pulled back her hood and peered at Sarah. She was wrinkled and could have been anywhere between seventy and a hundred years old, but that was not what was strange. No, it was her eyes that gave Sarah pause. Eyes that glittered like black obsidian glass. Penetrating and mesmerizing, they seemed to look right into her soul.

A shiver ran up Sarah's spine, but it was not in her nature to be impolite. "Please, be seated. Let me pour you some tea, and you must have a scone—they are delicious."

"You are too kind. That would be lovely."

After Sarah requested another teacup and plate from the serving girl and had poured and plated both tea and scone, she took a sip of her own tea and bit into her scone, sighing with pleasure. "There is nothing in the world that a good cup of tea cannot cure."

"I could not agree more." The old woman peered at Sarah over her teacup as she sipped. "Have you ever had your palm read?"

"What an odd question." Sarah shook her head and chuckled. "No. I don't really believe in that kind of hocus-pocus."

"Most people don't, but I enjoy dabbling in it. I find it very amusing, and some say I have a gift."

"Really." Sarah set her teacup in its saucer and slid her hand, palm up, across the table. "Amuse me, please." She had so many worries plaguing her, and she felt so indecisive, that any window into her future was worth considering.

Running away from Phillip and Waverly Castle was unlike her, yet she'd had no choice. How could she remain living there with so many obstacles between them? Not the least of which was how Society would look upon their living arrangements.

The discovery of her father's letter to Alfred was another obstacle that had shaken Sarah to the core. Learning that it was Phillip's father who'd caused her father's financial ruin and led him to commit suicide had left her so raw that she needed to put distance between herself and Phillip, if only to give her space and time to think.

But perhaps the greatest obstacle of all was herself. Even if Phillip did admit to having feelings for her, and even if she could somehow manage to get beyond the pain of knowing what his father had done to her father, there was the very real probability that she was barren. In the nine years of marriage to Alfred, she'd never conceived. She hadn't been too bothered by it in the first two years of their marriage, knowing that some women did not conceive right away, but by the third year, she would burst into tears each month when her menses began. She'd found it hard to speak of it with Alfred and pretended that all was well, when in fact she was heartbroken.

Keeping herself busy with her daily duties and nurturing her love for Alfred, Agnes, Patience, and Lizzie, she was able to come to some sort of acceptance that she would never have children. But everything changed when she met Phillip. Her feelings for him grew each and every day, and even if he returned her feelings, how could they possibly build a life together?

Regardless of her feelings for Phillip, she was the wrong woman for him. He needed an heir, and so did the dukedom.

Pulling her handkerchief from her pocket, she dabbed at her eyes, hoping the older woman would not notice.

Sarah needn't have worried; the woman was bent over her palm in complete concentration.

"What do you see?"

"Shush. I must ponder what I see and allow the vibrations to enter."

Sarah nearly pulled her hand away at the old woman's curt dismissal. She wasn't used to being shushed. She took a deep breath and controlled her annoyance.

"It seems you are running away, and you've caused someone a great deal of pain." The woman looked up, her black eyes scrutinizing Sarah.

She was taken aback by the fortune-teller's astute observation. "What I am doing is for the best for all concerned," Sarah said. She would not be judged by a stranger who knew nothing about her life.

"You have had difficulties in the past and lost dear ones who loved and protected you. There was also someone who failed you."

Sarah shuddered. The woman's words were eerily on target. *No, it's just a lucky guess. That could be said of anyone,* she thought. "Continue, please."

"There is a great love in your future. Marriage and happiness are within your grasp if you make the right choice. But if you don't, you will live out your days dissatisfied and full of regret."

"How will I know what choice to make?" *Am I actually paying heed to this charlatan?*

"I cannot say for certain. There is someone who will guide you, but you will have to trust that he or she has your best interests in mind. Do you know who this someone might be?"

Sarah's head was spinning. "I have not a clue."

"You have a long lifeline and will live into your old age. That's all I can see." The woman patted her hand before releasing it. She pulled a gold-cased timepiece from her satchel. When she opened it, an exotic melody poured forth, and Sarah could not help but wonder if the old woman had pilfered it from some gentleman's pocket.

She reached for her purse, pulled out a guinea, and set it on the table in front of the old woman. "Thank you for your time," Sarah said, getting up. "Our tea has cooled, and I would like a fresh pot." It was an excuse to catch her breath and be free of the woman's scrutiny, and when she returned with the serving girl in tow carrying a pot of hot tea, the woman had vanished.

Sarah's heart hammered in her chest. "Did you see her?" she asked the serving girl.

"See who, ma'am?"

"Never mind." Sarah sank into her seat and noted that the woman had not taken the coin. *Perhaps she was in a hurry to catch her coach, or perhaps I only imagined her.*

But for the rest of her trip to London, Sarah could not shake the old woman's words.

Chapter Ten

London, England
June 14, 1816

Sarah lowered her glass of sherry to the table. "So now you know my dilemma. I'm enamored with my deceased husband's nephew, and living in close quarters with him without Elizabeth has made it impossible for me to remain."

Sarah sat at a white linen-clothed table in Mrs. Dove-Lyon's office. The Black Widow of Whitehall and the dowager Duchess of Buckingham had taken to each other from the moment they'd met at the widow's birthday celebration. A friendship had blossomed, and now that Sarah had returned to London, she'd reached out to Bessie, and the two widows had made time to see each other regularly.

Sarah found Bessie to be a wise confidante who listened without judgment and whose sage advice was most prescient. The feeling was reciprocated, as Bessie admitted she rarely shared much of her private life with anyone. While the rumors surrounding her were good for business, they were not conducive to genuine human connection. But a true friendship with another intelligent woman who understood the complexities of life, as Sarah did, had been a welcome surprise. The two widows looked forward to their regular lunches at Mrs. Dove-Lyon's establishment.

"I understand completely," Bessie said, refilling their glasses from a fine crystal decanter. "The duke has no idea of his appeal. As upstanding as the man is, he's oblivious to the mores and improprieties of Society. Still, I often find men blind to what is right at the end of their noses." She'd removed the veil she usually wore as she made her rounds about the Lyon's Den. "As charming as they can be, they are also bullheaded and, in most cases, underestimate women in general."

"Exactly," Sarah replied, clinking her glass with Bessie's. "Although Phillip is cut from a different cloth when it comes to his estimation of women. He respected my advice when it came to the estate and business. But he sees no reason why we can't continue as we have before Elizabeth and the Earl of Dartmouth's elopement. He sees nothing wrong with spending days and evenings in each other's company, barely apart except for our beds." She took a sip of her sherry and sighed. "His logic is ridiculous. Like a typical male in that respect, repeatedly saying, 'Why do we care what others think?' A shortsighted reasoning if ever there was one."

"So true." Bessie nodded. "Men have no idea what women go through to protect their reputations."

"Exactly," Sarah said. "Because to suffer the indignity of *ton* gossip or be branded as licentious would be dangerous and injurious, not just to my reputation, but to my family as well. *His family*, I might add." She tasted a spoonful of the delectable lobster bisque. Bessie's cook was truly a wonder. The thick and creamy crayfish pottage was incredibly satisfying. "Besides, Phillip must marry and produce an heir, and then what?"

"I doubt any woman, not even a saint, would allow the beautiful young widow of the former duke to continue living in her household," Bessie said before taking a bite of crusty bread spread with the creamiest Irish butter.

"Nor would I wish to remain in the household with Phillip and his nubile young bride, fresh from her first Season. I'd be eaten alive with jealousy."

"Yes, I see your point. He should be thanking you for your foresight and fortitude. Good heavens, can you imagine what could have happened had you remained in that house one more day? You might have forgotten yourselves whilst sitting in front of the fire over a game of whist and given in to a moment of unbridled lust and passion."

Sarah's cheeks burned with heat. "Yes, and though I am ever cautious, my attraction to him poses a danger to my peace of mind. I am vulnerable to his charms. Thank heaven he has never acted inappropriately or without respect. I think the reason why he was so comfortable with our arrangement is because he doesn't share the same feelings for me as I do for him." She swallowed the sudden lump in her throat and reached for her water glass. Truth be told, that was at the heart of it all. *Why, for God's sake, does it bother me so?*

"Then it's good that you nipped it in the bud when you did and came to London. You both need the breathing room, I am sure."

"I haven't heard from him." Could Bessie hear the disappointment in Sarah's voice? It seemed she was incapable of hiding it.

"All the better." Bessie gave her a sly smile. "I think we need to put as much emotional distance between you and the duke as soon as possible. You, my dear Sarah, need a man in your life and, more importantly, in your bed."

Sarah nearly choked on her water. Bessie thumped her back and set the water glass back on the table. "Do not worry, my dear friend. I am not referring to a secret lover. Although wouldn't that be fun?" She winked. "We need to find you a husband. My usual matchmaking services are for women who've deservedly or undeservedly been burdened with a less-than-sterling reputation. They seek my services to find a man who can fulfill their expectations and help them reclaim their good name." Bessie patted Sarah's hand. "I will do this for you without charge."

"I will not hear of it," Sarah said, regaining her equilibrium. "I have more than enough to live a very comfortable life. As a businesswoman like you, I know that all services should be compensated."

"Very well, I will not quibble with you over money." Bessie gestured to her maid, who cleared the lunch dishes away. "You should know that the Sun King has asked about you."

"You mean James Harris, the Earl of Clarendon?"

"None other. The earl is a powerful man and an excellent prospect."

"Charming indeed, and quite suitable. I was not swept away by his attentions; however, in my experience, good feelings can grow with time." The earl had told Sarah at the masked ball that he had twin sons and a daughter. She would not have to worry about producing an heir to the earldom, which was a huge relief to her.

Bessie's maid returned with two delicate cups of gooseberry trifle. She set the desserts in front of them and quietly left the room.

A slight smile hovered on Bessie's lips as she dipped her spoon into the light and airy dessert and tasted it. "Mmm, this is wonderful. Do try some."

Sarah spooned up a taste and closed her eyes in delight. "Delicious," she said. She regarded Bessie, whose smile seemed to hide more than it revealed. She couldn't help but wonder if the widow was being completely candid with her. "Do you think me a fool to settle for anything less than true passion?"

"I know you have a practical mind, Sarah. And I know you must wonder whether passion can be sustained or if it's even necessary for a successful marriage. My experience has shown me two sides of the coin. Without the underpinnings of friendship and trust, passion tends to burn out. But I have also seen passion transform into something enduring and forever. Real love. But make no mistake, you and the

Earl of Clarendon would make a formidable couple, and I believe he would bring much passion to the relationship, even if you feel less for him. It's always better to be the one who is loved more."

Sarah laughed. "But, of course, you *would* feel that way, as you thrive on control."

"My husband left me destitute." Bessie's gaze swept the beautifully appointed office with its elegant Empire furniture and plush Savonnerie carpets. "He left me only this house, and it came with a mountain of debt. I scraped and scrabbled to build the Lyon's Den into the finest gambling palace in London. Yes, control is something I yield to no one."

"And so you shouldn't," Sarah said softly. "There is one more favor I would ask of you. Well, not exactly a favor, more of a business proposition. I will pay you to arrange a match for the duke. I fear he will never make an effort to find a bride. I sensed at your birthday celebration that you had someone in mind for him."

Bessie pursed her lips, considering. "There is a charming heiress with a slightly tarnished reputation whom he displayed some interest in before inheriting the dukedom. I think she might be amenable to such an arrangement."

Sarah did her best not to show her dismay at how quickly Bessie came up with a prospect. In truth, hearing about Phillip's interest in this mystery woman upset her more than the news that Bessie had someone in mind. Of course, he would have had many paramours as a soldier, and being as debonair and striking as he was, he would have attracted women everywhere he went. Why this upset her, she didn't know, but it was all she could do to beat back the tears.

"I would not wish on him someone who was not sincere in her devotion or one who lacked the heart or capacity to love him." Sarah did her best not to shirk Bessie's scrutiny. Indeed, she managed to meet the other woman's gaze straight on.

"I believe this woman could easily fall in love with the duke. The duke is exceedingly easy on the eyes. I, myself, find him quite irresistible."

Sarah wasn't sure what to think about the Black Widow of Whitehall's confession. But upon consideration, she realized Bess was right. *What woman wouldn't find Phillip desirable?*

PHILLIP JUMPED TO his feet like a schoolboy when he saw the carriage arrive, and then realized that, looking as he did, disguised as an old man, he might attract some curious attention. He glanced around Berkeley Square and was relieved to see that no one had noticed. Still, he couldn't control his thundering heartbeat as he watched Sarah step down from the carriage in front of Waverly House.

Damn, she looks beautiful. Sarah was elegantly dressed in a yellow worsted wool day dress trimmed with white ruffles, and her skin was a creamy ivory with just a pinch of color on her cheeks. She turned and surveyed the park. Her gaze fleetingly landed on him, and he slumped down, yanking the brown wool Homburg low over his forehead and hunching his shoulders in the heavy wool padded coat that made him look forty pounds heavier.

What would he do if she walked up to him and asked why he was sitting alone in the rain dressed like an old man? Fortunately, or unfortunately, she turned away, opened the gate to Waverly House, and walked up the steps. The butler opened the door and shut it behind her, and Phillip lost sight of her.

When had Sarah become his obsession? He wondered where she had been and whom she'd seen. Had she spent time with the Earl of Clarendon? Sarah had mentioned him in the past, much to Phillip's frustration. It had been bad enough to watch Clarendon, along with half the single men in London, dance with her at Bessie Dove-Lyon's birthday ball, but the thought of that damn rake courting Sarah made his blood boil.

But did he have a right to be angry over the possibility of Clarendon wooing Sarah? Didn't she have a right to be happy? He told himself that he could move on with his life if he felt that she had truly moved on to a new future. He might court a lovely young woman with an eye to marriage. Couldn't he? Although the thought of seeing her happy with the earl was enough to give him hives, what right did he have to spy on her? More importantly, why did he burn with jealousy every time he pictured the earl making love to Sarah?

Here he was, sitting in the park, across from their London townhouse, on a cold, wet, miserable day, watching Sarah from afar, when all he wanted to do was run across the grass, call out to her, and sweep her up in his arms. He dreamed of kissing her; maybe if he did, he could get over this obsession.

Not bloody likely, you miserable blackguard.

He missed her. It was like a visceral pain in his heart. He missed their conversations, the comfort he felt in her presence, sharing his meals with her, and most of all the humor that was so natural between them. He even missed her teasing him about his stubbornness and the lovely sound of her laughter when something she did or said left him speechless. But did he miss her because she had become such an integral part of his daily routine, or did he miss her for other reasons?

He rose from the bench and gripped his cane, hobbling down the street away from Berkeley Square. Phillip's thoughts churned as he walked to his carriage, parked a block away. Was it really just a year ago when his fortunes had changed? He was reminded of his conversation with the Gypsy fortune-teller:

"Do you have no interest in love, Your Grace?"

"Love is not what I aspire to at present."

"I see, but let me warn you, think twice before you decide what your aspirations truly are. Because if love presents itself and you resist, then it could be to your detriment."

Maybe love was what he needed. But was Sarah the woman for him? Here he was dressed up like an old man and spying on her, and to what end? She'd never given him any indication that she was interested in him as a future husband. Hell, she'd mentioned Clarendon often enough. And she'd picked up and moved to London without telling him in person.

Sarah was very clearly moving on with her life. She was a widow who wanted to remarry, and possibly have children. She was certainly young enough to do so. Phillip wondered why she didn't already have children. Had she not been intimate with the late duke? Phillip knew that some men, when they reached a certain age, lost interest in sexual activities. Had that been the case between Sarah and the late duke? God, he hoped he wouldn't end up like that.

It had been more than a year since he'd had physical relations with a woman, and he was about ready to explode out of his skin. There were only so many cold dunks one could take in the river, and only so many hours one could spend galloping around on a horse.

But was his attraction to Sarah so potent because of physical proximity? Was that why he had become so fixated on her? Was it because she had been the only constant in his life throughout all the turmoil and change of the past year? Sarah had always been there to talk to, to offer advice, share a joke with. But was that enough to build a life on? Was he chasing her and spying on her because he truly had developed feelings for her, or because of his own foolish pride in being unable to let go of a woman who'd become a dear friend? More than that, she'd become his best friend.

He couldn't think anymore. He needed a hot bath, food, and a diversion. The best place for him to lose himself and take his mind off Sarah was at the Lyon's Den. A little card play would stimulate his senses and take his mind off his troubling thoughts. A bit of distance and a proper perspective might spark some resolution to his dilemma. At least, that was what he hoped.

Chapter Eleven

London, England
June 14, 1816

Sarah entered the foyer of the townhouse, and after handing her coat, hat, and umbrella to Gibbons, she walked to the handsome console table, carved with acanthus foliage and husks, and decorated with a pineapple motif and urns. She opened the drawer, retrieving the day's mail.

"Will Your Grace take tea in the library?"

Sarah flipped through the letters and invitations until one caught her eye, and she turned it over to better examine it. Glancing up, she realized the butler was waiting for her reply. "I'm sorry, Gibbons, what did you say?"

"Tea, Your Grace—will you take tea in the library?"

"Yes, I could use a bit of warmth. The weather is simply abominable." The butler turned to leave. "Oh, and Gibbons, I fancy something sweet. A scone or two would be lovely." Sarah would have liked to curb her sweet yearnings, but she couldn't bear to forgo the pleasure.

"Yes, Your Grace."

A blazing fire in the hearth warmed the room. Sarah lit the oil lamp on the desk and sat down. After setting the rest of the mail on the blotter, she turned the envelope over. Breaking the blood-red wax seal, she slipped the expensive vellum paper out of the envelope and examined the handwritten invite. It was an invitation from the Earl of Clarendon to accompany him to a dinner party on Saturday at seven at Buckingham Palace, or, as it was affectionately called, the Queen's House. Was it possible that Mrs. Dove-Lyon could have had a hand in this, Sarah wondered? Even the matchmaker with her wily skills couldn't have arranged this so pell-mell. After all, Sarah had just seen Bess at the Lyon's Den an hour ago. But Bess did not suffer fools gladly, and she was the kind of person who moved with lightning speed. With mail being delivered twelve times daily in London, anything was possible.

Sarah penned her response and sealed the envelope with her Duchess of Buckingham seal. Until Phillip married and passed the seal to a new duchess, she was entitled to its use.

Gibbons entered, pushing a tea cart filled with all the trimmings. Sarah rose from the desk, holding her reply to the earl. "I will take my tea near the hearth. And could you please see that this is mailed today?" She handed him the envelope.

"Yes, Your Grace."

She poured a cup of tea and uncovered the basket of scones. "Thank you, Gibbons, and please tell Cook the scones look delicious."

The butler bowed and left. Sarah spread jam on a scone and served herself a generous dollop of clotted cream. Taking a bite, she purred with pleasure. The scone wasn't as good as Cook's at Waverly Castle, but it was a close second.

A thought occurred to her, and she frowned and stopped chewing the sweet delicacy in her mouth. Was it possible that the Black Widow of Whitehall had already arranged not only her invitation from the earl but also Phillips's match with a suitable bride?

No longer hungry, Sarah sipped her tea, washed the scone down, and sighed. She ruminated over the unsavory thought, realizing it was at her behest that Bessie acted, and she should bear no malice. It was what she wanted, wasn't it? Sarah had never been so confused, and felt like such a stranger to herself.

Saturday could not come soon enough. She needed to move on.

Alas, easier said than done.

Perhaps spending time with the earl would enable her to do that. He would undoubtedly be good company, and dining with Queen Charlotte would be a splendid diversion. The seventy-two-year-old queen had become more reclusive in recent years; however, she still fulfilled her duties as royal first lady and was a renowned admirer of music and a patron of composers such as Handel and Mozart. Queen Charlotte was not one to delve much into politics, so at least they would be spared that dinner table topic. And though her husband, George III, no longer fulfilled the duties of kingship due to his illness, Charlotte continued to function as the queen consort supporting her son, the Prince of Wales, even though they ostensibly opposed each other on most matters.

The prince regent and future George IV had assumed the power of the Crown in accordance with the Regency Bill of 1811. The king was in permanent decline and had officially been declared incapacitated. The regency was enacted, and the king's namesake and son, George Augustus Frederick, assumed the reins of power. George was king in all but name. Sarah wondered if he would make an appearance at Queen Charlotte's dinner party, but it was highly doubtful, as most of his time was spent with his mistress, Maria Fitzherbert, at either Carlton House or Steine House in Brighton.

Nevertheless, whether the profligate son made an appearance or not, for Sarah, it was a significant step in the right direction for her to be seen in Society accompanied by the earl, and she looked forward to it. Anything that kept her mind off Phillip was imperative. Anything that diverted her from missing Lizzie was a blessing. If Lizzie had written to her, she wouldn't know, as her letter would have been delivered to Waverly Castle and not to London. She would have to wait for Phillip to forward it to her—which, given the circumstances, might take some time.

PHILLIP LIFTED THE edge of the card he'd just been dealt and smiled. His luck had changed, as far as cards were concerned. The dealer revealed a count of twelve, and Phillip waved his hand, indicating he did not wish for another card. The masked dealer, Oberon, was beautiful and one of several women who had found honest work from a kind employer. The dealer pulled a king for herself, exceeding twenty-one, and Phillip won. Oberon paid him, and he doubled down on the next bet.

Tapping his fingers on the table, Phillip gazed up at the lady's gaming room and locked eyes with Penelope Chambers. He expected her to turn away and give him the cold shoulder the way she had before, but was dumbfounded by her beckoning smile. He stared at her, speechless. He couldn't fathom this change of heart.

At this inopportune moment, Mrs. Dove-Lyon chose to sashay up to him, her gaze following his to the lady in question.

"We have not seen you at our establishment in quite some time, Your Grace. Your luck seems to have changed in every way."

Phillip tore his eyes away from Penelope—to do otherwise would be unseemly—and found the Black Widow of Whitehall studying him. "I am unfazed and unchanged by my current circumstances. How have you been, Mrs. Dove-Lyon? Whatever time I have been away has brought no change to you. I might add that you are as lovely as ever, and no less observant."

Bessie laughed. "I have missed you and that charming way you have of diverting a question." She looked up and could see Penelope watching them. "I believe you have an admirer, Your Grace."

Phillip could feel his face redden, and he rubbed his hand against the shadow of a beard that had grown in since his morning shave. "Miss Chambers had no interest in me before I inherited the dukedom—why would I be inclined to find interest in her now?"

"One must be forgiving, Your Grace. Has it not occurred to you that everyone must answer to someone? In Miss Chambers' case, it is her aunt, Lady Isabella Carrington, who at the time would never consider you a catch for her niece. Since her father's death, the baroness controls the purse strings of Penelope's inheritance until she marries. It doesn't mean the young lady was disagreeable to your attention. In fact, I have it on good authority that Penelope was quite taken with you, but her aunt forbade her from encouraging you."

"Why would I want that woman interfering in my life? That aunt of hers is not likely to disappear into the woodwork. She will always be an interfering influence on whomever Penelope marries."

"Oh, come now, Your Grace. I know you well, and I've seen you admiring Penelope in the past, and now you protest at the possibility of getting to know her? And they say the fairer sex are the fickle ones."

"You are a wily one, Bess. You always have a reasonable argument. I admit it is one of your most endearing charms." Phillip thought about Sarah and her desire to start a new life and marry. If she did, where would he be? Miserable and alone. He looked up and met a smiling Penelope. He could do worse, he supposed. "And what of her reputation? I believe I heard rumors of a compromising situation with some Frenchman."

"All the more reason for you, a man of honor, to come to a damsel's rescue. She is comely and wealthy and longs to find true love and get out from under her aunt's machinations."

"I guess I have nothing to lose by spending some time with her. My mind has been so preoccupied with other things. A diversion might prove stimulating."

"Please join me in my office for a cognac, and we can discuss things further." Mrs. Dove-Lyon's bodyguard Bearnard cleared a path through the crowded gambling hall, growling at anyone who didn't move quickly enough out of their way. When he had delivered his mistress safely to her office door, he disappeared quicker than the last swig of ale in a drunkard's tankard.

Phillip had to hand it to the man. If he was anything, he was doggedly devoted. Phillip had known many a man like him in the army. They were always dependable on the battlefield, the kind of man you'd want covering your back. Bearnard might be intimidating, but Phillip appreciated how he protected his mistress.

Mrs. Dove-Lyon poured him a drink, and he sat back in a red velvet winged-back chair and sipped from a snifter containing a pour from a bottle of Napoleon Cognac from the Comet Vintage of 1811. Phillip had been in France and recalled seeing the comet in the night sky, where it remained for two hundred and sixty days. The comet's appearance coincided with a very long and hot summer that yielded the best grape harvest in years. Many considered the wines and cognacs produced from that harvest the finest in the world. He sighed as he inhaled the bouquet. "You do drink the very best, Bess."

"We only live once, Phillip. I believe in doing it well."

"I can't disagree with you." He held up his glass to salute her. "To the best! *À votre santé!*"

"Cheers! As I recall, you told me you grew up in France, did you not?"

"Yes, my father fled England after my mother's death. You, in fact, were one of the first friends I made when I returned to England after his death. I will never forget your kindness before I got my commission, and the war called me back to France."

"I would think with your perfect French, you must have been of special value to our military."

Phillip never spoke of his time in France during the war, except on occasion with Sarah. But never did he talk about his reconnaissance behind enemy lines. He'd been sworn to secrecy, and there was no good reason to dig up the past. Phillip had paid dearly, losing his eye. Returning to that time produced an anxiety he tried his best to avoid.

A knock at the door saved him from answering Bessie's question.

"Come in," she said.

The door opened, and Bearnard waited for Penelope Chambers to cross the threshold before closing the door behind her. Phillip wasn't surprised to see Penelope. It was, after all, what Mrs. Dove-Lyon had been driving at when she asked him to join her for a drink. He rose from his chair respectfully. The young woman seemed not nervous, and he assumed she was aware of and agreeable to Mrs. Dove-Lyons's machinations.

Penelope held her hand out, and he took it, bending to kiss it.

"Your Grace," she said in a breathless voice. "It is a pleasure to see you again."

The scent of her perfume ambushed his senses. "The pleasure is mine, Miss Chambers."

He released her hand, and she turned to her benefactress. "How nice of you, Mrs. Dove-Lyon, to arrange a meeting between me and the duke."

"I am always happy to bring people together," Bessie said. "One never knows what will come of it. Will you excuse me a moment? I must check on something." Her gown rustled as she swept from the room before either Penelope or Phillip could reply.

Penelope chuckled. "It seems we have been abandoned."

"If you would prefer, I can find someone willing to chaperone us."

"I feel no need—that is, if you are comfortable being left here with me?"

Phillip sat in his chair and waited to see what she would do. After a glance around the room, she sat in the chair next to his.

"I heard of your good fortune and want to congratulate you," she said. "You must be very pleased with how things turned out for you."

He eyed her with curiosity and a fair measure of distrust. "Yes, very pleased indeed."

She looked down at her hands, which were clasped in her lap. "I imagine you are wondering why I never showed interest in you before. I hope you can forgive what must seem rather duplicitous on my part. You must think me shallow, and I can't blame you. But I hope we can get past these ill feelings and perhaps make a new start."

It was brave of her to admit the indifferent manner she'd treated him before he became a duke. If he did not wholly forgive her, the door opened a smidgen. His negative feelings toward her abated enough for him to treat her with civility. "I am not a man who holds a grudge, so I am open to making a new start." He smiled, hoping she would know he was sincere.

"Wonderful." Penelope's shoulders relaxed, and she looked infinitely pleased. "I am invited to a dinner party Saturday evening at the Queen's House. I wonder if you would accompany me. It is sure to be a stimulating evening, but I'd rather not go alone. It also would allow us to become better acquainted."

Phillip's first instinct was to say no, but he restrained himself. What was he going to do, sit outside on that damn bench, torturing himself, watching Sarah come and go? Seeing her dressed to the nines for a night out on the town would plunge a dagger into his heart. *By Jove, I will not wallow away in self-pity.* What he needed was to try to move on, just as Sarah had.

"It will be my pleasure to escort you, Penelope."

"Then we have an understanding to let bygones be bygones?"

Maybe not entirely, but certainly for one evening. "We do."

CHAPTER TWELVE

London, England
June 15, 1816

SARAH LOOKED OUT the window of the earl's elegant landau as it drove through the gates of Buckingham Palace. The horses smoothly carried the carriage through an archway to a circular drive that gave entry to the Queen's House. The king had purchased Buckingham House as a family retreat in 1761, and fourteen of the king and queen's fifteen children were born there.

The renovated palace of stone and brick had been converted to a three-story French neoclassical design. Compared to other European royal houses, it was modest, but to Sarah it was still imposing. An iron-railed fence enclosed the property, and as the carriage approached, every window was alight with glowing candles and gas lamps. Members of the royal guard stood at attention. Others marched around the grounds in ordered rows or rode horseback wearing brightly colored cavalry uniforms, their heads topped with plumed helmets and bearskin caps. The might of England's regiments guarding their queen was a sight indeed. But the soldiers barely noticed as the guests stepped down from their carriages and entered the palace.

For the occasion, Sarah had worn the sapphire and diamond necklace and earrings Alfred had bought her in Paris, and she wore the same black velvet gown she'd worn for her portrait hanging at Waverly Castle. Never inclined to waste, she'd had her modiste alter the gown to reflect current fashion, and it boasted full, puffy sleeves that displayed her shoulders and an empire waistline that accented her lily-white décolletage. Her hair was drawn up into a loose bun of red curls held in place with a black velvet ribbon and pins.

The earl had beamed with pleasure as he watched her descend the staircase at Waverly House, and had made much of how beautiful she looked. Sarah knew he was proud to be escorting her, and it tickled her fancy.

She turned to the earl. "Do you know how many guests are attending the queen's soiree this evening?"

He took her hand and kissed it. "This evening's guests will not number more than twenty, I suspect." He chuckled. "An intimate gathering for a monarch, but the queen enjoys a gathering of old and new friends. She misses the happy days when the sovereign did not suffer from the affliction that stole his mind." He cleared his throat. "I was so pleased to hear of your return to London, Sarah. I hope you are open to my calling on you so we may better get to know each other?"

"Thank you, James. You compliment me with your attention. To not welcome your friendship would be impolite and ungrateful of me."

"Dash politeness. I am a lucky man to be welcomed into your company. A more beautiful or intelligent woman does not exist in England or on the Continent. I am honored to know you."

The earl was a dignified man, and this evening was a lovely treat. If only she felt a spark of passion for him or a weakening of the knees when he smiled at her as she did with Phillip. It was unfortunate, but not for a minute did she wonder what the press of the earl's lips on hers would feel like, nor did her mind wander to the bedroom, where visions of lying in the embrace of a dark-haired man haunted her dreams.

She refused to acknowledge that that man was Phillip, who, while she slept, did scrumptiously wicked acts that awakened her in the dead of night covered in perspiration and left her weak from unfulfilled desire. She'd taken to bathing in cool water every morning, just to soothe her heated flesh. It seemed she would have to resign herself to the reality that all was unfair in love and war, because it was the earl and not the duke who kissed her hand, and it was the earl in whose company she found herself.

"I will not discourage your attention, James. I am honored."

Sarah pulled her cloak tighter around her, glancing upward at the sky, where clouds blocked the moon and stars. It was hard to imagine that the entire summer might come and go without a sunny day or a starry night, but it was possible. She recalled Phillip's dire predictions of the climate effect from the volcanic eruption.

Phillip... On an evening out with a suitor, she shouldn't be thinking of him. *I will not think of him.* And with the greatest of effort, she banished him from her mind. *Be sensible, Sarah, and appreciate the man you are with.*

Sarah handed her coat to the footman, smiled at the earl, and looped her arm through his. They followed the footman to a reception room, where a server greeted them holding a silver tray offering flutes of champagne. James handed her a glass and toasted, "To you, my dear."

"Thank you, James." She touched her glass to his. "To us."

"Indeed," he said, taking a glance around the room. "Come, let me introduce you to our fellow guests." He led her to a group of men and women clustered together, laughing.

Seeing their approach, one of the gentlemen in the group said, "Harris, where have you been, old man? I haven't seen you at White's lately." He held his hand out to shake, and his gaze shifted to Sarah. "And who is this lovely lady accompanying you? Does she have any idea what she's getting herself into, being seen with a scoundrel like you?" Everyone in the group turned their attention to the earl and Sarah.

The woman next to the man admonished him with a tap of her fan on his coat sleeve. "Behave yourself, Robbie."

"Thank you, Jenkinson, for your vote of confidence," the earl said with a chuckle. "Pay him no mind, Sarah; he's just the prime minister and of no real consequence. Fortunately for him, he married up, as they say." The earl bent and kissed the hand of the woman who'd scolded the prime minister. "May I present Her Grace the Duchess of Buckingham, Sarah Farnsworth Villiers? Sarah, I want you to meet the far more interesting half of this couple, Countess Louisa Jenkinson, whose acquaintance I know you will enjoy making. Oh, yes, I nearly forgot the disagreeable gentleman beside her is Robert Jenkinson, second Earl of Liverpool and our current prime minister. Lord, have mercy on us all."

Everyone chuckled at James teasing the PM. The earl continued with introductions to Arthur Wellesley, the Duke of Wellington, and his wife Catherine, who appeared fragile and timid. Rumors abounded that Wellington and Catherine's marriage was not a love match, and from what Sarah could see at a glance, the stories were true. Wellington looked at her in a most unseemly way.

The third couple appeared the exact opposite—Cameron Tidings, the Earl of Broadmoor, and his wife, a woman half his age, who was referred to as Sweetums and who giggled at whatever anyone said. These two behaved like besotted newlyweds, based on the puppy-dog look in his lordship's eyes when he looked at her and the way Sweetums held tight to his arm.

Everyone attending the dinner party knew each other, and the relaxed familiarity among them dispensed with the formality inherent in Society gatherings. Getting a few jibes in was accepted with grace and good humor.

Sarah wondered if the dinner conversation would become more serious and take a political bent. But then again, she doubted the men would consider political discourse proper at a social gathering with women in attendance. She had long been rankled by the dumbing down of conversation when women were present, but nothing could be done about it. Women, regardless of the strides they were beginning to make, were still treated as chattel. Sarah keenly followed the issues taken up by Parliament. She was grateful that her husband had been progressive in his views about women. She supposed it had much to do with his having three daughters and no sons.

Sweetums giggled, and her eyes lit with adoration. "I still haven't gotten over last month's celebrations. I don't believe I've ever seen a more beautiful or happy bride than our Princess Charlotte at her wedding, have you? She and Prince Leopold are a dazzling couple."

"She is a fine lady," said Jenkinson, "and will be a wonderful queen one day."

Princess Charlotte was, after her father George Augustus Frederick, next in line for the throne. Considering that the queen had twelve living children, it was worrisome that there was only one legitimate descendant in the line of succession. Of course, everyone knew of the many illegitimate children sired by Charlotte and George's sons. It was whispered that their third son, Prince William Henry, had ten children with his mistress, the actress Dorothea Jordan. It was a juicy tidbit of royal debauchery often referred to in the scandal sheets.

Sarah sipped her champagne, entertained by the guests' gossip and interactions. She said little, finding it far more interesting to observe. It was evident that Prime Minister Jenkinson greatly admired his wife and her opinions. He deferred to her in conversation, and Sarah imagined that Louisa had played an essential role in her husband's success.

She recalled a quote from one of her favorite poets, Robert Burns: *A woman can make an average man great, and a great man average.* She wondered if that observation was accurate about the prime minister and his wife. Sarah believed that a strong woman who was an equal partner in a marriage made a stronger man.

Sadly, it was easy to see the opposite between Catherine and the Duke of Wellington. It was such a blatant mismatch, which was far more common in Society than a love match. It only served to remind her of her own plight. If she married without love, would she, too, become a shadow of her true self? It was demoralizing to think that one's life was in the hands of fate.

"I say," said Jenkinson, "I believe that is Penelope Chambers on the arm of a man I'm not acquainted with." Everyone but Sarah turned to look, and the PM waved the couple in to join them.

Louisa whispered in Sarah's ear, "This is the first time we've seen Penelope in public since her dalliance with the French diplomat. It isn't fair how men can break all the prescribed rules of Society and get away with it, but a woman faces ruin if she, heaven forbid, steps out of line."

"How are you, Penelope?" asked Catherine. "We have not seen much of you this season."

"I am wonderful, Louisa," Penelope replied. "My aunt has kept me busy commuting back and forth from London to Maplewood, her estate in Pembroke. Do you know my escort, Phillip Villiers, the Duke of Buckingham?"

"But of course," said Wellington. "He served heroically and was a trusted officer in the service of His Majesty and part of my inner circle in our war against the French. I haven't seen you since Paris, my friend. It's jolly good to see you, Villiers."

"It is good to see you too, sir," a deep baritone voice replied.

Sarah's heart nearly leaped from her chest when she heard Phillip's name, and the familiar cadence of his voice caused her composure to take flight. She turned slowly to face the couple and found him regarding her with a frosty look.

Her pulse pounded in her ears, and she heard nothing of what was said until Phillip spoke. "The duchess and I are well acquainted," he said in a clipped voice. "After all, she was my uncle's wife, and we spent some time together when I claimed my inheritance. She taught me a great deal during the short time we both resided at Waverly Castle. I haven't seen her since she decided to live in London." He took her hand and bowed, pressing his lips to her hand. Heat flushed her neck, traveling in a slow burn to her cheeks.

Everyone looked at Sarah, and she knew she must respond, but her mouth felt dry, and her head was spinning. She'd tried so hard to push Phillip from her thoughts, and seeing him looking more handsome and commanding than ever in his dress uniform made her knees tremble.

"Your Grace, thank you for your kind acknowledgment," she said, "but you took to your duties like a duck to water. I'm happy to have played a small part in your taking the reins of the dukedom." She glanced at the inquisitive faces, her heart stampeding in her chest. "Now, if you'll forgive me, I must powder my nose."

Remembering the earl, she turned. "I shall return in a few minutes, darling." Her inflection on the endearment and her hand on his coat sleeve were purposeful, in the hope of conveying more intimacy than she felt.

Phillip's burning glare followed her as she swept through the room as if being chased by hounds. Her pulse pounded in her ears, and with every step, she was sure she'd never make it from the salon without stumbling and falling.

Once safely out of sight of the guests, she made her way down a long hallway. But her head spun, and she was forced to steady herself. With one hand on a console table and the other gripping the velvet skirt of her gown, she paused to calm her racing pulse. *Take even breaths,* she told herself. *He may hate you now, but one day he will realize it is for the best.* Tears filled her eyes. *Drat.* She wiped them away. Now, she really was in want of a good nose powdering.

The ladies' retiring room was magnificent, with full-length mirrors, a plush red carpet, crystal sconces, and a chandelier. A maid was present to assist female guests with any unforeseen catastrophes, such as spills, dress repairs, or the re-pinning of their hair. There was much to take in and admire, but Sarah was not in any frame of mind to do so. All she wanted was to flee the palace and not be made to look into Phillip's censorious gray eye. For once, she was grateful he didn't have two eyes, as it would have been doubly distressing.

Stop it! She hated herself for even thinking such a cruel thought; if she could, she would have done anything to restore his other eye.

How would she make it through an entire evening being so near to him and having to bear the contempt written all over his face? How dare he make her feel so uncomfortable? She blamed Mrs. Dove-Lyon and her matchmaking schemes, even though she knew it was at her behest that Bessie had acted. *Damn the woman for being so efficient. The only solution is to ignore him and his withering stare. I will not allow him to ruin my evening. Hah, as if he already hasn't.*

Sarah powdered her face in the mirror above the vanity and applied rouge to her lips. Regaining her confidence, she asked the lady attendant where she might get a breath of fresh air. She was led to a set of French doors that opened to a small patio surrounded by gardens.

The perfume of night-blooming jasmine scented the air, and she filled her lungs. It was chilly, and without a wrap, she soon felt the cold on her shoulders and trembled. She turned and saw an imposing figure blocking her entrance to the palace. She shuddered. The darkness prevented her from seeing who he was, but, of course, she knew.

CHAPTER THIRTEEN

London, England
June 15, 1816

PHILLIP WAITED A few minutes after Sarah's departure to excuse himself. He was determined to speak with her. Seeing her in that dress, looking more beautiful than he'd ever seen her, had stolen his breath away. It was impossible for him to spend the entire evening pretending to be interested in Penelope.

All eyes were on him as he strode from the room, but he didn't care. He was bombarded with visions of the first night he'd seen Sarah, how taken he'd been by her then and every day that followed. It was the dress she'd worn in her portrait. Seeing her in that dress stirred him to the point of pain and made him want to grab and kiss her for all the world to see.

Her laughter rang in his ears, and he was reminded of how often she'd taken him to task for his seriousness and inability to laugh at himself. In those moments of her lighthearted reprimands, he would find himself fighting an impulse to fall to his knees and beg her forgiveness.

It was unseemly, but he wanted to bury his face in her skirts and inhale her scent. At times it felt as if he were going mad.

My God, I love her!

He was in love with Sarah. He'd probably been in love with her since the moment he met her—correction, from the moment he set eyes on the portrait of her hanging at Waverly Castle. Love had always been the furthest thing from his mind, and now it was all he could think about.

Seeing Sarah was like a punch to his solar plexus; the vision of her sucked the oxygen out of the room and made it difficult for him to breathe. His emotions ran havoc over his sensibilities, leaving his stomach tied in knots. Seeing her with the earl had lit a match beneath him and set his heart afire with jealousy. The tangle and intensity of his emotions exploded in a conflagration that threatened to consume him. He needed to regain his self-control over what he said, what he did, or what he should do.

How damaging would it be to his good name if he misspoke—but more worrisome, how harmful would it be to Sarah? The only way to douse the fire burning inside him was to speak to her in private.

He had to bare his soul and confess how much he missed her, how life had become a tedium of tasks with no light on the horizon to warm his future. His thoughts were jumbled, but he had to tell her the truth—the realization that he was truly in love with her. That he couldn't bear living without her.

Not sharing breakfast with her or dining with her at the day's end made the days lackluster. More importantly, hers was the only face he wished to see when he rose in the morning, and in truth, it was the only face Phillip longed to see in his bed before he fell asleep. A vision of her glorious hair splayed across his pillow plagued him day and night.

He was like a caged lion with a thorn in his claw; she was the only person on earth who could remove it and end the agony. The only way forward was to tell her what was in his heart.

He strode down the long hallway, straining to hear the creak of a door, the rustle of her gown, anything that might reveal where she was. The hallway was dimly lit by crystal sconces and candlelight. As he searched for her, he thought about how best to explain that his world no longer turned smoothly on its axis, and she was the reason. His life and devotion to God, country, and king felt unimportant and worthless, as if he'd wasted his entire life on meaningless exploits. Now he found himself devoid of a compass and lost to himself. He could no longer disabuse himself of the truth; she was all he thought about. Even worse, she was all he dreamed about.

He'd come to London to see Sarah, but in his wildest dreams, he hadn't expected to come face to face in such a public situation. *Damn you, Bessie.* This was happening because of Mrs. Dove-Lyon and her matchmaking schemes. She'd convinced him to give Penelope Chambers a chance, and if not her, to at least open himself to the idea of finding a suitable woman to be his duchess.

He'd succumbed to the Black Widow of Whitehall's reasoning and persuasive skills, even though he knew Penelope was not what he wanted. How could he betray his heart and fool himself into thinking he could ever love her or anyone else? And now here he was in a royal palace, risking all, searching for the woman who'd run away from him without a care for the pain it might have caused him. *Why in God's name does she not realize, even without my saying so, the depth of my feelings?*

Phillip caught the fragrance of Sarah's jasmine perfume and followed the scent like a foxhound hunting a fox. He was so intoxicated just knowing she was near that he froze when he spied her through the French doors, standing by herself.

For a moment, as if on cue, the clouds parted, and she was bathed in moonlight. He held his breath, afraid to disturb the vision. He wished he was an artist and could capture the iridescent play of moonlight on her red hair and alabaster skin so that he might gaze at her forever.

Though he wished time would hold still and he could observe her for a bit longer without her knowing, it couldn't last, and Sarah turned toward him, clearly sensing a presence.

Her breasts rose with her gasp, as heat and desire raced through his veins; though it was cold and damp outside, Phillip was on fire. The way Sarah stared at him made him realize she couldn't see him as he stood in shadow.

"Don't be afraid, Sarah—it's me." He stepped fully into the moonlight. "I'm sorry if I frightened you."

"Your Grace, you startled me. Why are you here?"

He took a few steps closer to her. Pain squeezed his heart that she would address him so formally. "Do you mean here in London? Here at the palace? Or here outside with you?"

She shrugged her perfect shoulders that he longed to run his fingers over. Better yet, if he could only take hold of them and pull her fully against his length... Then, before she could protest, he would silence her by crushing his lips against hers and fulfilling his need with a deep kiss. He pictured her emblazoned from his passion, willingly submitting, and responding wholeheartedly with that wildness of spirit that he longed to see. If he could contrive or write the scene, that was how he saw it playing out.

Instead, she shook her head, and a smile of forbearance lifted the lips he longed to kiss. "You need not be specific, Phillip. I wouldn't want to pry into your personal life or your motivations. They are not any of my concern."

He couldn't stop the rueful burst of laughter. "Come now, Sarah, we both know that isn't true. There is nothing in my life that I haven't shared with you over the course of our knowing one another. I have kept no secrets."

The sparkle in her eyes suddenly faded, and he didn't understand why. "Not everything. In fact, there is something that had a ruinous effect on my life that you knew about but failed to tell me of." She shivered and rubbed her arms.

She's freezing, you fool. His worry for her instantly extinguished the questions he thought to ask, and he removed his scarlet tunic and draped it around her shoulders. Whatever she referred to could not have any consequence in the scheme of things. Some slight he inadvertently caused should not be discussed here or now.

"I have no idea what you're referring to, but you're freezing. I can't allow you to catch a chill while we resolve this." He rubbed her arms as he searched her eyes for any softening of her manner. She didn't squirm or make a move to pull away, and for a long, drawn-out moment, they stared into each other's eyes.

Dear Lord, I am lost. There was nothing he wouldn't do to win her favor.

After what seemed like an eternity, she whispered, "Your Grace, please don't do this."

"Do what?" He could not fathom what, to his mind, sounded like an expected response, when in truth, he sensed an underlying plea for him not to stop. *I know she feels our connection. The magic that reverberates every time we touch.*

"You have put yourself and me in a compromising situation. If we are discovered—"

"I don't give a damn who discovers us. I care only about you and me. Why must I pay heed to anything or anyone that comes between us? Do we not deserve to pursue our desires and our happiness?"

"We cannot resolve this here, and you have no idea what my desires are. There is a young woman who awaits you and a good man who, at this moment, is surely wondering where I am. Please, I cannot breathe with you so near."

"And I have not taken a breath since you left." He bit back a rueful chuckle at the bitter irony and truth. Sarah must have felt his anguish, for her gloved hand gently caressed his cheek.

"We are a sorry pair, are we not?" she said softly.

"It doesn't have to be this way, Sarah." His voice sounded raspy to his ears. Her touch ignited him. The only thing comparable was the elation after taking a dose of laudanum, which, in a depressed state, he'd tried after losing his eye. He remembered the experience of being in a pronounced state of euphoria. That was what being with Sarah did to him: she made him soar with joy. Happiness. Something he'd never truly known in his life.

"How else can it be?" she asked.

"You could return to Waverly Castle, and we could figure this out." *Dammit! Why can't I just say what I'm feeling?*

Anger flashed in her eyes. "I will not." She removed his coat and handed it to him. "Let us hope the queen is not cross with us for not being there when she makes her entrance." And with that, Sarah spun around and disappeared, leaving him more bereft than before.

He hadn't told her he loved her, which was what he'd intended to do, but the truth was this was not the place or the time. He did not relinquish hope, nor would he give up. Sarah might think everything that needed to be said had been said, but she would be wrong. He would convince her. He would know no peace until he did.

CHAPTER FOURTEEN

London, England
June 15, 1816

WHAT IS HE thinking? Sarah blinked back the tears that filled her eyes and clenched her fists. *I'd like to wring him by that obstinate neck of his!* Why had he come to London? Was it just to disrupt her world? Did he not have a clue as to the way she felt about him? *Men are so blind, but none blinder than he.*

In the back of her mind was always the letter. She was still in shock over what her father had written to Alfred. How would she get past the most significant hurt she'd ever experienced? Phillip's father had destroyed her world and altered the course of her life.

How could she contemplate a life with Phillip, knowing what his father had done? Even if he had no knowledge of his father's sins, he was his son. His father's blood ran in his veins. How could she bear to look at him across the breakfast table, let alone sleep in the same bed, knowing that his father had caused the downfall of her father? Knowing that her father killed himself because of what Phillip's father had done?

Oh, God, if only I didn't crave his touch the way I do.

How could she keep denying the truth? Her heart had been lost to Phillip long ago, and even knowing what his father had done could not erase her feelings.

Sarah returned to the ladies' retiring room to compose herself. Looking in the mirror once more, she powdered her cheeks, hiding the physical proof of her tears.

But I can't hide the pain in my heart.

Even if she and Phillip could put the past behind them, there was still the very real possibility that she was barren. How could she even contemplate a future with Phillip, knowing she might not be able to give him children, an heir? At least with Clarendon she wouldn't have to worry. He was a widower with three children—twin boys and a girl by his late wife.

Sarah was no fool. She knew James was not only seeking a wife, but a mother for his children. If she did marry him, she would be a second wife again, and a stepmother again. But at least she would know the joys of mothering younger children.

Taking a deep breath, she returned to the salon, where several new couples had arrived. James pinned her with a worried frown. "Are you all right, my dear?"

"Yes, perfectly fine. I just needed a breath of fresh air."

"The queen rarely makes an appearance until every guest has arrived. Of course, it is a monarch's prerogative to make a grand entrance."

"I'm ever so glad she is not yet here, as I would never want to be the cause of any offense." From the corner of her eye, she saw Phillip return and join Penelope. She had only a moment to contemplate their interaction before a footman announced the queen's arrival.

The queen entered, leaning on the arm of Princess Sophia, one of her many unwed daughters. They were followed by a distinguished-looking gray-haired man whose lapel was decorated with medals and commendations. James whispered that the man was a diplomatic envoy from the Duchy of Brunswick and Lüneburg. Count Schoenberg was a visiting member of the German branch of the Hanoverian family, representing the close bloodlines between the royal houses of Europe. The king and queen were descended from the house of Hanover, as was nearly every other royal personage in Europe and Russia.

Waiting for the queen to make her way around the room and greet everyone, Sarah was shocked to see how much older Charlotte looked. She had heard that the queen turned gray overnight when King George began to suffer from mental dysfunction. Charlotte had never been a beauty in the classic sense. Still, she'd always behaved regally, and her devotion to the king was much admired. Her love of family had gained the respect and goodwill of the people of her adopted homeland.

Sarah could well understand the problematic hand that life had dealt the queen. Her husband's bouts of insanity were legendary, and it must have been heartbreaking that the king and queen's sons had fathered so many children, with various mistresses and wives, who would never be recognized as legitimate. To date, only one granddaughter, Princess Charlotte, who was recently wed, would, God willing, ascend to the throne.

Sarah felt sorry for Princess Sophia, who was nearly forty years old and had never been allowed to marry because of her father's illness and her mother's need for companionship. It was whispered she had given birth to an illegitimate son, the love child of the man in charge of the king's horses, Major-General Thomas Garth. Sarah couldn't imagine how heart-wrenching it would be to give up your child, which Sophia had no choice but to do. One might believe being royal born was an easy life, but nothing could be further from the truth.

She curtsied to the queen and Sophia when James introduced her. "Your Majesty, how do you do?"

"I am well, thank you. The earl has informed me that you lost your husband not long ago."

"Yes, ma'am. It will be two years in October."

"How difficult it must be for you, my dear. I met your husband, the duke, many years ago. I remember he had a wonderful sense of humor and a lively mind. He and my George had a spirited conversation."

Sarah smiled. "Thank you. Were he alive, he would be pleased to know you felt that way, Your Majesty."

"A good marriage is a gift from God. I remind myself of this every day. Do I not, Sophia?"

"Yes, Mama, you do, and we all thank you for it." The window into Sophia's mind opened momentarily, and what Sarah saw was heartbreaking. Sadness and regret shone in her eyes. The emotions were gone as quickly as they appeared, and Sarah wondered if she hadn't imagined it.

"To be grateful for what one has or has had is the only way to live one's life," the queen continued.

"Yes, ma'am. You are most wise." Sarah was struck by the queen's bravery in the face of her troubles. But she also wondered what harm the royal parent had caused her children by keeping them tied to her apron strings.

Charlotte nodded, and Sophia led her away to greet the other guests. One of Sarah's fears was put to rest. She'd heard the queen spoke with a heavy German accent, and worried she might have trouble understanding her. Queen Charlotte did not speak English when she arrived in England to marry the king. But though her English was heavily accented, she was quite understandable.

The earl whispered in her ear, "I believe the queen was quite taken with you. I expect you will be invited back for tea or luncheon."

"Princess Sophia appears so unhappy," she whispered back.

"I'm afraid being royal is not all it's thought to be. I am sure that never marrying or having children to nurture is a profound loss to the princess."

Sarah fanned her face. What the earl said could be applied to her too. She had no children of her own, and no husband, and the years were flying by in the blink of an eye. As for developing a relationship with the queen, although it would be an honor, Charlotte lived in a world entirely apart from hers, and court life held no interest for her.

She heaved a deep sigh behind her fan. She was finding it increasingly difficult to focus on anything else with Phillip nearby. The one time her eyes had strayed to him, his gaze was firmly fixed on her, even as Penelope engaged him in conversation. It shocked her that he could behave so brazenly. But a part of her could not help the heat that spread like wildfire throughout her body from his smoldering stare. She fluttered her fan, trying to cool herself down, and tried to beat back the surging desire that was threatening to engulf her.

Dinner was finally announced, and the queen and Sophia led the procession of guests to the dining room. Formality was *de rigueur* at the palace, and protocol was followed with exactitude. No one began their meal before the queen consort, nor did anyone eat after she laid her utensils down after finishing each course. Praise the Lord, the queen was a slow eater, so at least no one would leave the table hungry.

Sarah was relieved that Phillip and Penelope were seated at the other end of the table, and she wouldn't have to endure a conversation with them, as one did not engage in conversation at the table with anyone other than those on your left or right. But there was no way of avoiding Phillip's furtive glances, even though she tried her best not to look at him. Adding to her discomfort were the awkward moments when James discussed state matters with Louisa and the prime minister, which often coincided with the German diplomat seated on the other side of her being engaged in conversation with Sophia, leaving Sarah with no one to speak with. Feeling conspicuous and without focus, she found her gaze roaming the room, enduring but not enjoying her evening.

The queen excused herself shortly after the meal and retired to her rooms. The farewells were short, with many promises of getting together in the future.

James hinted at sharing a possible nightcap as he escorted her home, but Sarah didn't invite him in, professing a headache.

"Are you sure you're all right, my dear?"

"Yes, perfectly fine. It's this abominable weather."

"It has cast a damper over the season's activities. May I call on you this week? If the weather clears, perhaps we might enjoy a ride in the park."

"That would be lovely, James."

She bussed him on the cheek and sighed in relief when Gibbons shut the door behind her.

"Gibbons, I believe I will have a sherry in the library."

"At your pleasure, Your Grace."

Gibbons stoked the embers in the fireplace and threw another log on the hot coals. Sarah could not help but wonder if it would ever warm up enough during this horrid summer to give the fireplaces a rest. The butler poured her a sherry from a crystal decanter and set both glass and decanter on the table next to her. "Will there be anything else, Your Grace?"

"No, thank you, Gibbons. I will be fine. Goodnight."

"Goodnight, Your Grace." The butler bowed and quietly closed the door behind him.

Sarah kicked her shoes off and curled her legs beneath her. She sipped the sherry and contemplated the evening. It was no good pretending otherwise—her attraction to Phillip was as great as ever. If she thought running away to London would bring closure and allow her to move on, she was mistaken.

I may need to go farther away. Distance and time away from him might be the only solution.

It crossed her mind she should write to Lizzie and join her and

Lucien in Italy. But the thought of imposing herself on their honeymoon was entirely unthinkable. She needed advice, and the only person she trusted besides Lizzie was Mrs. Dove-Lyon, whom she sensed would not betray her.

Yes, I will do just that; I will visit Bessie tomorrow. Indeed, she will help me decide on a course of action.

PHILLIP STARED AT the flames in the fireplace and sipped from a snifter filled with cognac. The hotel was far from the flat he'd rented when he first returned to London. It was also a far cry from the luxury of his townhouse, where Sarah was ensconced at this very moment. He longed to be there with her, and wondered if she felt as sleepless as he did.

Do women like her believe in love? He couldn't answer that question with certainty, even with everything he knew about her. He sensed that her marriage had been about loyalty, trust, security, and companionship, but had lacked passion. Given the age difference between the late duke and Sarah, it was understandable.

Did she even care about that? He couldn't imagine that the woman he felt so passionately about didn't wish to feel the same way. She might never have felt that way before and didn't understand what it meant.

Don't be a fool. And never underestimate her. Even if she's never felt it before, she vibrates with it. What would it be like to awaken her passion?

Heat settled in his loins, and he was wont to stop the fire that burned below his belt. He had never known such desire or frustration.

Then something Sarah had said tonight thundered in his brain like a warning shot over the bow of a ship. *"There is something that had a ruinous effect on my life that you knew about but failed to tell me of."* It bothered him that he had no idea what she was talking about.

Why didn't she discuss it with me? Why the subterfuge? Is this the real reason she ran away? He had to get to the bottom of this, or they would never find a way forward. *But what is forward? Will she even consider marrying me?* He could not bear the thought of her refusal.

What to do? What to do? He tapped his fingers on the mantel and stared at the flames as he repeated those words in his head like a mantra, hoping to find clarity. He'd failed in his attempt to tell her how he felt. When did he become such a coward? Was it so hard to admit aloud his feelings for her?

Use your military discipline and come up with a strategy. This isn't so different than conquering the enemy. What are the obstacles, and what stands in your way? Mrs. Dove-Lyon must be put off the case. She must stop.

There was no way in hell he would have Bessie matching him up with every available woman in London. Tomorrow, first thing, he would give her notice that he was no longer on the Marriage Mart. Then he would convince Bessie that her collaboration was in the best interests of everyone involved. The Black Widow of Whitehall must help him with Sarah.

Could he trust her? The more Phillip thought about it, the surer he was that Bessie would be the perfect accomplice. Her experiences had perhaps jaded her, but he suspected her matchmaking business meant more to her than money. She was a woman who understood love and believed that two hearts could be destined for each other. He was determined, and sensed Bessie would believe in his quest to conquer Sarah.

It was like a battle cry within him: *Omnia vincit amor!* Love conquers all! He had to keep that thought foremost in his mind. Tomorrow he would do battle. To triumph was ingrained in him, and never was it more important than now.

Chapter Fifteen

London, England
June 16, 1816

Sarah raised her teacup to her lips. She was sleep-starved, and no amount of face powder could hide the dark circles beneath her eyes. Thank goodness Mrs. Dove-Lyon had the grace not to mention how poorly she looked.

"Did you know that Penelope invited Phillip to the Queen's House last evening?" Sarah asked nonchalantly.

Bessie's face revealed nothing as she placed her teacup in its saucer. "No, I simply arranged their meeting—set the stage, so to speak. I did not involve myself afterward." A smile tickled her lips. "Oh my, the two of you at the same event with escorts. Hmm, that must have been amusing."

"Amusing? It was one of the most uncomfortable gatherings I have ever endured."

"Oh, come now. You are both grownups and capable of civil behavior in public. Neither of you is in a committed relationship, nor did you have a real falling-out before this encounter. The queen is kind, and you must have met some interesting people. What could possibly have gone wrong? And what of your blossoming relationship with the earl?"

"Yes, yes, the people were fascinating. As for the earl, he's very accommodating, but I'm afraid I bear no feelings for him beyond friendship. What ruined the evening was Phillip's behavior. It was most unseemly."

"How so?"

"He had the temerity to follow me when I went to seek some air."

Bessie's eyes sparkled with interest. "Did he? And what did he say to you?"

"Some nonsense about our being allowed to pursue our desires and happiness. I have no idea of what he was alluding to."

"You did not ask him to clarify? Perhaps he was befuddled by the situation."

Sarah furrowed her brow. "Why would I encourage him? And it was he who sought me out. Whyever would he be befuddled?"

"He's a soldier, Sarah, and voicing aloud one's feelings may not come easy for him."

For a moment, Sarah contemplated Bessie's answer. Should she tell her about the most traumatic period of her life and her father's letter? It was so painful to admit and such an embarrassment to reveal. What good would it do? She doubted she could ever surmount her anger at what his father had done. Although it was unfair to harbor anger toward Phillip, she could no more forget the injustice his father had done her than forget how to breathe. And what of her barrenness? The thought of sharing the greatest tragedy in her life made her stomach turn over. How could she allow anyone to know of her defect?

A knock on the door interrupted her thoughts. Mrs. Dove-Lyon put her teacup down and bade them enter. The behemoth of a man who guarded the widow poked his head in.

"Bearnard, is there a problem?" Before the man could answer, Phillip pushed past him into the room. Bearnard grabbed him by the collar and was about to yank him out when Mrs. Dove-Lyon intervened. "That will be all, Bearnard. Please unhand the duke. Mercy me, is every man in London seeking to do battle?"

The bear of a man growled but released Phillip, who turned and straightened his collar.

"Bearnard, I would never want to meet you in the ring," he said with a grin, "but I appreciate your devotion to your mistress."

"Watch your step, Your Grace. I am not impressed with your title or your antics. If you need me, m'lady, you need but call." Bearnard grunted at Phillip and shut the door.

Mrs. Dove-Lyon asked, "What have you to say for yourself, Your Grace?"

Sarah had jumped up as Phillip had stumbled in. Anger now colored her cheeks. "Phillip, what is the meaning of this? Are you following me? Was it not enough that you nearly brought ruin on both of us at last night's dinner party?"

"Sarah! I must speak to you."

"Whatever for? How dare you behave in such a volatile manner? You embarrass both of us. First, you follow me outside at the Queen's House, and now you follow me to the Lyon's Den!"

Mrs. Dove-Lyon rose. "I see this is a personal matter that should be resolved in private. I shall leave you two alone to work this out."

"No, please stay, Mrs. Dove Lyon," said Sarah. "Whatever the duke has to say, I'm sure he can say it in front of you."

She was sure Phillip was losing his mind. In the time she'd known him, he had always been calm, with an exacting level of self-discipline and self-control, no doubt from his years as a soldier. But lately, his behavior had become completely erratic. She could not imagine what had gotten into him. But whatever it was, she needed to put him in his place. She would not be stalked or monitored by him. He was not her husband, nor was he her keeper.

"Do not say things we will both regret, Sarah. I came because of a situation of great urgency. I received a telegram this morning that there's been a fire at Waverly Castle. I have no idea what the damage was or if anyone was seriously injured. Nor do I know if the fire reached the stables. Henry's telegram was brief, simply requesting I make haste to Buckinghamshire."

The blood drained from Sarah's face. "Oh, dear God. I apologize, Phillip, for my hasty accusations. Of course you were right to find me. We must leave immediately for Waverly Castle and see what can be salvaged from this catastrophe."

"I'm glad you agree. I fear Henry did not convey the worst of it, nor who may have been injured, or worse. If the stables caught fire…" Phillip's voice cracked.

Sarah reached for his hand. "You're thinking of Lysistrata and Pegasus. I cannot bear the thought. We must hurry."

"I'm so sorry," said Mrs. Dove-Lyon. "Can I do anything to help?"

"Thank you," Phillips said. "I hope I speak for both the duchess and myself in saying how we appreciate your offer, and will keep you informed."

"Yes, of course," added Sarah. "I will see you are kept apprised." She embraced Bessie, and Phillip's brows rose with surprise. She'd expected as much, as he didn't realize how deep her friendship with the Black Widow of Whitehall was. The cat was out of the bag, and nothing could be done about it now.

In any case, nothing mattered besides their getting to Waverly Castle, or what was left of the ducal estate. She would not give in to her fears. They would return and do what needed to be done.

Slipping her cloak around her shoulders, she made for the door with Phillip close on her heels.

Sarah moved with purpose through the Lyon's Den. "The ducal carriage is parked just down the street," she called over her shoulder.

"If you drop me at Waverly House, Sally and I will pack posthaste. You can gather your things from wherever you are staying and return to fetch me."

"Aye, the sooner we leave, the better."

Once underway, they spoke only about what should be done when they arrived in Buckinghamshire. Since worry dominated their conversation, nothing of a personal nature was broached.

"I'd hoped you would return with me," said Phillip, "so I took it upon myself to telegraph Buckingham Inn and reserve two rooms for us. I hope you don't mind my assumption that you would want to assess the damage for yourself."

Sarah patted his hand. "Of course not. Waverly Castle is my home, and the family home of Agnes, Patience, and Lizzie. Everyone's welfare there concerns me. I would have insisted even if you had suggested I needn't accompany you. I am grateful you chose to inform me of this calamity. I would have been terribly upset if you hadn't."

"Whatever it takes, Sarah, we will make this right. I will rebuild Waverly Castle regardless of the damage. You will have your home back."

"Oh, Phillip, Waverly Castle is your home as much as it is mine."

He nodded. "Indeed, I have come to see it as such."

How she wished she could sit next to him and feel his arms around her. But thinking of that made her yearn for more than just comfort.

She must have somehow transmitted her thoughts to him, for he regarded her with an intensity that nearly took her breath away. Her cheeks burned with a blush as a sudden heat surged between her thighs.

"Are you feeling well, Sarah? Your face is flushed." His voice's lower register caressed her like a bow across the strings of a cello. The stimulation made her body taut, as if his fingers were pressed against her fingerboard. It wasn't hard for her to imagine what it would be like to be played as if she were an instrument by Phillip. The very idea stole her breath and produced an unseemly trembling that she tried to hide.

Her breath escaped in a rush, and she fidgeted and looked out the window. "I'm fine. I'm just worried."

He took her hand and pressed his lips to it. Did his mouth linger longer than was usual, or did she imagine it?

Releasing her hand, he whispered, "We are both worried but mustn't assume the worst." He looked out the carriage window. "We've arrived. If it is agreeable with you, I will return for you in an hour. There is no time to waste." He jumped out of the carriage and held her hand as she stepped down.

"I will be ready." She turned and left him. Sarah cast her fears aside. Phillip was right—worrying did nothing to help the situation. She had too much to do and little time to do it. She breathed a sigh of relief, happy to focus on something other than her inner turmoil. The way she felt about him was something not within her control.

Sarah knew the days ahead would be emotionally trying and require a level head, but resisting her heart's desire would not be easy. She prayed that the fire had not reached the stables and that no one was injured. And she also prayed that some part of Waverly Castle had survived. She wiped away the tears that filled her eyes as she thought about the memories, paintings, and treasures representing the history of the illustrious Villiers family that may have been lost. *Irreplaceable.* But these objects were nothing compared to their valued staff and tenants and their families, or their beloved animals.

Speaking of animals, she must see to Potsy's care, as she could not bring Lizzie's beloved pet with her.

"Sally," she called. "I need you!"

Sarah's lady's maid came running down the stairs. "Yes, Your Grace?"

"I must pack immediately; there is no time to waste. I need sensible clothing and shoes and nothing formal." Sarah ran up the stairs past Sally. "Gibbons, please bring my portmanteau to my room. And make haste. I am leaving for Waverly Castle. There has been a fire! I will explain everything to Sally while we pack, and she will inform you of what I know. I will send word to you later, but hurry. The duke will be here shortly to pick me up. Pray for everyone in Buckinghamshire."

CHAPTER SIXTEEN

Buckinghamshire, England
June 18, 1816

It was dark by the time their carriage arrived at the Buckingham Inn the following day, and it had begun to rain, the nasty weather continuing its summer assault. Phillip helped Sarah from the carriage, and the doorman held an umbrella over her as they hurried inside. There was no use making the trip to Waverly Castle tonight, as it would be too dark to assess the damage.

Phillip checked them in and sent a message to their butler Henry, who was staying temporarily at the groundskeeper's cottage, for him to meet them in the morning. Nothing could be done that night. Sarah needed dinner and freshening up from the four-hour journey from London to Buckinghamshire. She had insisted they not stop, her anxiety about getting there overriding any concerns for herself. She'd wanted to go directly to Waverly Castle but acquiesced to his suggestion that they wait until tomorrow.

The innkeeper led them upstairs to their rooms on the second floor, which, he assured them, were the best at the inn.

"I'm sorry, Your Grace, for this misfortune, but be assured we will see to the comfort of the duchess and yourself."

"Thank you, my good man. We are forever grateful for your accommodation and support."

"It is nothing, sir. Everyone in the township is ready to do whatever is needed. It is well known that we have always been well served by His Grace, the late duke, and you are now carrying on that tradition. I will see that your bags are delivered to your rooms immediately."

"Sarah, you must be famished," Phillip said. "Would you care to have a bite with me? I'm sure Mr. Grange can have the inn's cook assemble something for two weary travelers."

"Not a problem at all, Your Grace. I am sure there are mutton, potatoes, and pudding aplenty. If you'd like, I could bring meals to your room—"

Sarah cut the innkeeper off in mid-sentence. "Thank you, but I am far too tired and worried to eat." She turned to Phillip. "If you don't mind, Your Grace, I only want to unpack and sleep."

Phillip was sure the displeasure on his face was there for all to see. Sarah, however, pretended there wasn't anything amiss, ignoring his frown. He was also annoyed at her reverting to addressing him formally, even though he knew it was proper for her to do so in front of the townsfolk. He would not, however, give her the satisfaction of addressing her with the same formality.

"As you wish. I suggest we breakfast at eight and leave for Waverly Castle immediately thereafter."

"That is acceptable to me. I bid you goodnight, Your Grace. And thank you, Mr. Grange."

The door to Sarah's room shut, and Phillip couldn't help but feel dismissed. He didn't understand why she was distancing herself so completely from him. He tied himself into knots trying to understand her. He'd been harboring a hope that being in Buckinghamshire would soften her demeanor toward him.

In the coach, she'd been amiable whenever they spoke, but the minute they arrived at the inn, she'd built a wall between them. Yes, there was the awful prospect of what they faced tomorrow, but wasn't it better to face what was ahead together? For him, being in her presence, the comfort of knowing she was near, was enough to withstand whatever life threw at him. Why did she not feel the same?

Maybe she does, but letting on would bring down that damned wall standing between us, and she is too stubborn to let that happen. Well, I have news for you, my lady: I will not retreat. The time will come sooner than you think when you and I will reveal our hands.

It occurred to him that he would be happy to live in isolation and never interact with another human being again so long as he could live his life in the company of Sarah. He didn't need Society, and he didn't need the dukedom, for that matter. What he needed was to be with her. He was determined to embed himself in her heart, no matter how long it took.

Sarah loved Waverly Castle, and to live there with her for the rest of his life would be heaven on earth. Phillip knew he would have to speak the words aloud for her to understand the depth of his feelings. How ironic that it took her leaving for him to realize that depth. Now, the only thing Phillip was sure of was that he would not let her return to London without telling Sarah he loved her.

Not just loved her, but loved her more than life itself.

THE NEXT MORNING dawned with heavy black clouds, which could only mean more rain. Sarah and Phillip breakfasted in the inn's pub, which was permeated with the scent of day-old ale and smoke. They both drank black coffee and ate sausage and eggs, served with what Phillip suspected was last night's potatoes. It didn't matter what was served; given what they faced when they reached Waverly Castle, neither of them had much appetite. A distracted Sarah pushed her food around her plate, and though Phillip had a hearty appetite, his worry about what they would find at the castle diminished his hunger.

"Did you sleep well?" He did his best to engage Sarah in conversation; anything to lift her from the silence that she wore like a shroud. "I understand how difficult this is, but it is unlike you, Sarah, not to see your way out of the abyss that has stolen your positive nature. If you would only confide in me what you are feeling, we might find our way to overcome whatever troubles you."

The anger in her eyes sent a shiver down his spine. "To what purpose, Phillip? What good can come of my confiding in you? You and I are on different paths, and ne'er the two shall meet. It isn't healthy for us to expect more from our relationship."

"Is that what you really think? Don't you realize how dear you are to me?"

"Am I?"

"Can you not see it? Do you not know it? For God's sake, I turn to you in any crisis."

"Is our so-called relationship based on crises? Is that what we're about?"

Phillip ran his fingers through his hair in frustration. "Stop twisting my words and get to the point. Just say it. You don't share the same feelings for me that I do for you."

She stared into her coffee cup and whispered, "I would be lying if I said that."

"Then don't shut me out, my darling." It was an admission, if a small one, that she cared, and he took heart. He hoped the endearment he used would make her realize what she meant to him.

Instead, the curtain lowered, and he could not read her expression. "Is it not time we left? We will not solve anything between us now, especially with what this day may have in store for us. I think it would be better to keep our emotions in check."

Her suggestion was sensible. Sensible Sarah, as always. But she was right. "Very well, but I assure you this conversation is not finished, and I will broach the subject again."

She sighed and lowered her cup. "I would expect no less, though I wish you would leave well enough alone."

"It is not my nature to leave well enough alone. A man must follow his beliefs and do what he knows is right."

"No, I suppose leaving well enough alone isn't in your nature."

His lips twisted into a smile as she purposely misconstrued his meaning.

"I believe I meant not pursuing what is right is against my nature," he said.

"Have it your way."

"I most certainly will." He chuckled, and finally, the stony edifice on her face cracked into a smile. It was as if the sun's rays had just burst from a cloud, showering radiance and warmth on him. Happiness swept through Phillip in a wave, swelling his chest and every other muscle in his body, including one he would rather contain.

It was miraculous what a tiny smile from her did to him. Nothing and no one had ever produced such an exquisite rush of feeling, and he fought to control himself from shouting to the rafters that he loved her.

Steady, man. Now is not the time, not yet—but soon.

TEARS RAN DOWN Sarah's face as the carriage approached Waverly Castle. Plumes of smoke rose from the smoldering ruins. Chimney stacks of brick stood naked and blackened by soot, looking like tombstones rather than the last surviving sentries of the once beautiful manor. Her heart skipped a beat—the stables appeared untouched. It was the only hopeful sign in an otherwise bleak landscape.

She laid her hand on Phillip's. "It looks like the stables may have been spared." She wiped her eyes. "The house seems completely gutted," Sarah whispered.

"Don't despair yet, my dear. Let's wait to speak with Henry." He pointed at the two men standing near the front façade of the manor. "There are Scotty and Henry."

The carriage stopped, and Phillip hopped out, offering his hand to her.

"Your Graces, I am sorry to welcome you back to Buckinghamshire under such dire circumstances. I wish it were otherwise."

"Thank you, Henry, and a good day to you, Scotty, although I can't see anything good about today," Phillip said. "Please explain what happened. Was anyone hurt?"

Sarah couldn't speak as she stared at the smoldering piles of wood, glass, furniture, and what was left of the gold frames of treasured paintings scattered across the blackened ground. The air was thick with ash-laden fumes, and she held a handkerchief to her nose.

"We are not sure where the fire broke out," Henry began. "It was four days ago, in the evening, after all the staff had gone to bed. I woke up to the smell of smoke, and the main floor of the house was on fire, making it impossible for us to get down the stairs. We tied sheets together, climbed out of a window, and slid to the ground. I'm afraid Cook lost her grip and fell, breaking her leg."

Sarah gasped at the news. She adored the older woman whose kindness was as renowned as her talents in the kitchen.

"Cook is made of stern stuff, my lady," Henry said. "We drove her to her sister's in Akeley to recover, and we'll send someone tomorrow to find out how she fares, but I daresay it will be long before she'll be needed back here."

"Thank God Cook is all right," Sarah whispered, dabbing her teary eyes. "I will plan to visit her when we've assessed the damage here."

"I will take you myself," Phillip said softly.

"Thank you." She took a deep, shuddering breath. "What of Lysistrata, Pegasus, and the rest of the horses and animals? Dear God, please tell me they are safe."

"Aye, they are, Your Grace," Henry replied. "When the fire broke out, George, fearing it would spread, ran to the stables and released all the horses and animals, who raced for the open pastures. We rounded them up yesterday, and the horses and livestock are with the tenant farmers. I'm afraid we've lost most of the chickens, but we were lucky with the other animals."

Sarah nodded, grateful that the animals had been rescued and the staff had all survived.

Phillip patted Henry on the shoulder. "Don't worry—I intend to rebuild Waverly Castle. We will build it bigger, better, and more secure than it was before. In the meantime, you should know that everyone in the employ of the dukedom will be taken care of, and your positions will remain for you. I would appreciate your spreading the word about that."

"Thank you, Your Grace. I will see that everyone is notified."

"You, Henry, and you, Scotty, of course, I will need throughout the rebuilding."

"Scotty, what of Elizabeth's glasshouse? How did it fare?" Sarah asked.

"It is a complete loss, I'm afeared," Scotty replied. "The glass could nay withstand the heat. We were unable to save any of the plants or fruit trees."

"Oh no!" Sarah covered her mouth. "Lizzie will be devastated."

"We will rebuild the greenhouse, too," Phillip said. "It will give Lizzie and Lucien a reason to visit us often."

The lump in Sarah's throat stopped her from responding. Hearing Phillip allude to her living at Waverly Castle in some distant future was eviscerating. It would be unlikely she'd live in Buckinghamshire ever again, and the thought tore her apart.

She tuned out the ongoing conversation between the men and surveyed the grounds. She didn't know what she could hope to find amid the ashes and fallen timber, but something caught her eye. She stepped away from the men and, keeping to the outside footprint of the foundation, walked around to get a better look.

Sarah didn't know what it was, but it drew her like a magnet. To find a treasured memento among the ruin that was once her home seemed like a miracle to her, and she couldn't stop herself from retrieving it, even if she had to wade knee-deep in muck. A quick glance over her shoulder told her Phillip's back was to her, as he, Scotty, and Henry were intent on their discussion.

She tentatively made her way through the debris. Lifting her skirt, she stepped over large pieces of charred timber strewn across what was left of the foundation. Her boots sank into the rain-wet ash. The shiny object was not of her imagination, not some trick of the light, and she knelt and grabbed hold of a tarnished chain and pulled, lifting it and its pendant free.

She gasped, unable to believe what she'd found. It was a gold locket—her mother's locket. Her father had given it to her when she was old enough to appreciate its worth. Her most cherished keepsake. She had no idea why she'd left it behind, other than she'd been in such a rush to leave for London that she or Sally must have forgotten to pack it.

She rubbed it against her dress, cleaned it as best she could, and ran her finger over the engraved initial F. With trembling fingers, she opened the locket, and her eyes widened. Somehow the likenesses of her mother and father, commissioned by her father at their engagement, had survived the fiery inferno. Tears streamed down her cheeks, and she gently snapped the locket shut and pressed it to her heart. As far as she was concerned, it was a good omen, perhaps even a miracle.

She turned to make her way out of the muck and caught her heel on something. Her arms flailed as she fought to recover her balance. Phillip's shout, "Sarah, be careful!" filled her ears, but she fell backward, and her head slammed against something hard. Terrible pain engulfed her before darkness overwhelmed her.

Chapter Seventeen

Buckinghamshire, England
June 20, 1816

P HILLIP HAD NEVER prayed more in his life than he did for Sarah to wake up. He sat hunched over, his elbows resting on his knees. For two days, he hadn't left her bedside. Why hadn't he noticed her heading toward the ruins? He would have stopped her, *should* have stopped her, but it was too late by the time he paid heed and called out to her to be careful. She'd slipped and fallen, hitting her head on a large supporting timber, the thud so loud that it pierced his heart like a dagger.

He'd run to her and scooped her up, shouting for the carriage driver. She was unconscious, but at least she was breathing. In an instant, his panic turned to determination, and then years of experience from the battlefield kicked in. He moved her quickly from the danger, as he'd done for so many other wounded comrades, climbed into the carriage, and cradled her in his arms, ordering the driver to make haste back to the inn.

What had she been thinking to take such a risk? It was far too dangerous to scavenge among the ruins. And what for? Some worthless piece of jewelry that even now she clung to, her fingers locked so firmly around the object that he couldn't pry it from her grasp. It was beyond his understanding why she would risk her life for this pittance. He would buy her whatever jewelry her heart desired if only she would come back to him.

Phillip studied her face, so pale, so still that she resembled a beautiful statue. He was in utter despair that he might lose her without declaring his love for her. He didn't know how he would go on.

Over the past two days, the doctor had come and gone numerous times but accomplished nothing. Sarah lay in a state of unconsciousness that the physician said was caused by a concussion, which he explained was a shaking of the brain.

What he said had only exacerbated Phillip's anxiety. "Surely you can do something. You *must* do something!"

"There is nothing we can do for her. She will either wake from this coma or she will not. But I must warn you, even if she regains awareness from this deep unconscious state, she may bear permanent damage. There is no way of predicting how much of her brain was affected or the neurological impairments that might arise. She is in God's hands."

"I will do whatever it takes to care for her. I will not lose her."

The physician had lifted his brows, as he knew the dowager duchess was not Phillip's wife, but Phillip didn't give a flying fig for what the man thought. Reputation be damned.

He hadn't slept a wink since, his one good eye was rimmed red and bloodshot, and now it was evening. He dared not sleep for fear that she might regain consciousness and he would miss it.

Sarah lay on the bed in a fetal position. The physician had suggested she not lie on her back, as it would put too much pressure on the large lump at the back of her head. Every hour Phillip applied cold compresses to the swelling, careful not to press too hard against the stitches where her head had hit the wooden beam.

A soft sigh escaped her lips, and Phillip leaped from his chair and knelt by her bed. She had sighed last night, and he'd hoped it was a sign that she was waking up, but it wasn't. Still, he would not give up hope.

Lifting her hand in his, he whispered, "Sarah, my darling, can you hear me? There is so much I want to tell you, so much that is in my heart." He studied her face for a sign that she could hear him. "I have been a complete and utter oaf. I should have realized that you, as an honorable woman, could not possibly continue to live with me at Waverly Castle after Lizzie and Lucien left for their honeymoon. But I was only thinking of myself, and my own stubborn pride. I didn't care what Society thought. But I should have cared. I should have realized." He caressed her cheek with his hand.

"Oh, God, I was such a fool. I should have gone after you right away. And even after I followed you to London, still I hesitated. I should have courted you in the way that you deserve. I should have told you, my beautiful Sarah. I should have told you how much I love you.

"I think I fell in love with you from the first moment I laid eyes on you. But I—I didn't realize it. I was too stubborn to see it at the time. Too stubborn to share my feelings with you, thinking we would go on together as we were, living and working side by side. Every time I opened my mouth, it always came out wrong somehow, and now, here I am finally telling you, and you're so far away...

"Please don't leave me, my beautiful Sarah. Please don't leave me alone in this world without the only one I will ever love."

He bent and pressed his lips to her hand. Tears streamed down his face, and he could taste the salt on his lips. "I've made such a mess of things, but I promise I will make amends, if only you'll come back to me. Please tell me it's not too late. Give me a chance to prove what you mean to me." He bowed his head, pressing his forehead to her hand, and wept.

He sat by her bed and continued to talk to her until his voice had gone hoarse, and even then, he continued to whisper endearments until, exhausted, he fell asleep, his face pressed to Sarah's palm.

Phillip was riding Pegasus and Sarah was riding Lysistrata across meadows, side by side. The wind danced through her red hair, and her laughter pealed like the bells of Christ's Church in Buckinghamshire. The sound was enough to set his pulse racing.

They stopped in a secluded meadow, near a brook. He helped her down from her horse and slowly peeled away her clothes, until she was standing before him gloriously naked. Smiling, she tugged on his hand and pulled them down to the blanket he'd thought to spread out. There, in that meadow, he made love to her, and only when she reached the pinnacle of pleasure did he lose himself inside her. His shouts of rapture joined with her breathless cries of love.

The dream was so real that he could feel her fingers in his hair, the delicate touch so wonderful that a groan escaped him. It was always the same whenever she touched him. When her hand rested on his arm when they took a walk, or when he helped her down from the carriage, or when she brushed against him in some unplanned manner. As always, a current flowed between them, something unexplainable that ignited and held him, binding him to her.

As consciousness came to him, he smiled. It was unexplainable, but he could still feel Sarah's fingers in his hair. *I can feel her hand. How is that possible?*

His eyes flew open as hope burst from his heart, and he lifted his head to gaze into her beautiful sapphire-blue eyes—only to see they were still closed. But then he saw her smile. Her beautiful smile. She was smiling as her fingers were softly moving through his hair. His heart raced, but he dared not stop the miracle from unfolding.

"Sarah," he whispered hoarsely. "My darling, have you come back to me? Will you not speak to me?"

Her smile deepened the dimple in her cheek. He wanted to shout his joy to the rafters but was afraid that perhaps he was still dreaming. The thought wrenched his heart.

"Please, my darling, will you open your eyes?"

"Why did you call me darling?" Sarah's whisper made him nearly jump out of his skin. "What happened, and why is my head throbbing?" Her eyes opened, and he didn't know whether to laugh or cry.

"How do you feel, my darling?" He kissed her hand.

"Not terrible, except for the pounding at the back of my head. I will live, won't I?"

"Yes, you will live and return to your charming self. I am grateful my prayers have been answered."

Sarah studied him. "You haven't answered my question. Why are you calling me darling? Isn't that a tad much for what we are to each other?"

Seized with daring and a need to reveal himself to her, he dived in. "You are everything to me, Sarah, and I cannot live without you."

Color filled her cheeks, and it thrilled him. "Phillip, I know we are friends even when we disagree, but please don't say things you don't mean."

"I'm not addled, regardless of my lack of sleep." He lifted her hand and opened her fingers, revealing a gold locket. He held it up so she could see it clearly. "You fell retrieving this." Sarah looked at the locket, and he could see she was trying to remember. "You hit your head and were knocked unconscious. You've been in a deep sleep for two days."

"Is that why you look so terrible? Have you slept at all?"

"Not really." He rubbed the whiskers on his cheek. "Truth is, I've been out of my mind worried about you. The physician wasn't very reassuring. You have stitches, and that bump on your head had to be iced. I wouldn't leave you and never trusted your care to a stranger." Phillip's gaze dropped to the locket. "Did Alfred give it to you?"

Sarah inhaled a deep breath, and her body stiffened. The change was unexpected, and he couldn't figure out what had upset her. He watched her fingers shake as she pried open the locket. She didn't add any commentary or explanation. A tear slid down her cheek, and then she handed the locket to him.

It was no use asking her what was wrong; she wanted him to look at the miniature portraits on either side of the locket. His first impression was of a man with dark hair dressed stylishly in a high-collared white shirt and hunter-green waistcoat. Opposite was a miniature of a beautiful redheaded woman whose face was eerily familiar. When he looked closer, the beat of his heart ratcheted up, and confusion overtook him. He vaguely recognized the man. He'd seen him before, but where?

Sarah broke the tension. "You know him, don't you?"

"I-I'm not sure."

"Think hard, Phillip. You know what became of him. What you didn't know is his connection to me. He is—was—my father. He committed suicide when he faced financial ruin, which is how I came to live at Waverly Castle. Alfred Villiers and Roger Farnsworth, my father, were best friends. I found my father's letter to Alfred, his farewell to life."

An uncomfortable prickle climbed Phillip's spine; his heart raced as realization dawned on him. Sarah's words to him at the queen's dinner party thundered in his head.

"There is something that had a ruinous effect on my life that you knew about but failed to tell me of."

It was as if he was emerging from a dense fog. He cleared his throat. "Your father lost his fortune due to mismanaged investments. But what has this to do with me?"

"Phillip, delve deeper into the past. I believe you know, but you purposely refuse to see the truth."

He scrubbed his face with his hands to grasp where she was leading him. "My father lost his way after my mother died. To survive, I'm afraid he did business with unscrupulous individuals. I am not excusing his despicable behavior. I had no knowledge of what he was doing, having taken a commission in His Majesty's service. My father left a trail of ruined lives that I did not discover until my return from war."

"But you recognized my father's face," Sarah whispered.

"I do. I recall seeing him with my father. I came in at the tail end of their conversation, as he was leaving. He didn't mince words and blamed my father for luring him in with promises of making a fortune. It was evident that they had known each other for a long time, and that was it—your father left in anger. I did not know his identity, and I didn't ask. I felt horrible, but there was nothing I could do. As I told you, my father left a trail of broken dreams and financial ruin in his wake."

Sarah rubbed the lump on her head and winced.

"Are you all right, my darling? Isn't it better we leave this conversation for another day?"

"You still don't see it, why you and I can never be?"

"You're not thinking straight, Sarah. There is no reason for us not to be together. I have loved you since the first moment I saw you. Fool that I am, it took me longer to figure it out and tell you."

"Stop! Don't you see that I bear an intense malice toward your father, and if we were to be together, one day, that hatred might transfer to you? I cannot bear to be the cause of your unhappiness."

"That is ridiculous. You can no more hate me than hate God." He took her hands in his. "Admit it, you feel the same as me. I felt it in my gut, I knew it in my soul, but you, too, refused to admit it to yourself. We were both blind and denied what was right in front of our eyes. Tell me it isn't true." The love he bore her nearly overwhelmed him. He desperately needed to bridge the gap between them and tear down the walls she was determined to erect. He would no longer be put off.

Sarah's eyes dropped to the gold locket. "I will not deny my feelings for you. What I will deny is furthering them."

"Look at me, Sarah. Look at the man who would sell his soul to the devil to make you his."

She placed her finger on his lips, silencing him. "Do not say such sacrilegious things."

"Why? It's true. I'll continue to say it for the rest of my life. I love you, Sarah Farnsworth Villiers, and I will never love another." His arms gently encircled her, pulling her against him, and before she could protest, he dipped his head, meeting her lips. Phillip refused to be denied. If she pushed him away, it would pain him, but he would never stop trying.

Her response was twofold—she returned his kiss, and her body went pliable against him. Her kiss exploded a sensory revolution that changed his life forever. When breathlessly they broke apart and stared into each other's eyes, he saw tears in hers.

"My darling, do not think or talk yourself out of what we both want. Follow your heart and marry me as soon as you are recovered. Together we will rebuild Waverly Castle and build a family. I don't care if our wedding causes a scandal. You will be my wife for the rest of our days, and I will honor you and protect you. But, my darling, you must find forgiveness in your heart for those who have wronged you. Only then will you find peace. Carrying this grudge against the dead will only bring you sorrow. Believe me, I know. I almost died on the battlefield, I lost my eye, but I could not allow the anger and bitterness to fester in my soul. Far braver men than I lost their lives. I was one of the lucky ones. The best day of my life was not the day I found out about my inheritance—it was the day I met you, my darling. I love you, Sarah, with every fiber of my being, and that will never change.

"I know that my father hurt your family. He hurt my family too. But I am not my father. I am my own person, just as you are your own person. We cannot allow the mistakes our parents made to define who we are in life. I rejected my father's choices and found my own path.

Believe me, I will do everything in my power to make you happy. I live for the day that you will bear our sons and daughters."

He held her hand in his, hoping he was getting through to her. "You and I together can make this right and find redemption in our love. You are my family, you, Elizabeth, Patience, and Agnes. You are the light that guides my way. Please don't turn away from our love, for it is precious."

He waited, trying to read her beloved face. Never, even on the battlefield, had he felt as if his life hung more in the balance.

WHEN PHILLIP KISSED her, all her best arguments disappeared like clouds blown away in a windswept sky. Instead, powerful sensations took root in her that she could no more deny than the ridiculous notion that men and women were not different. Wisdom and experience told her otherwise; besides, she'd been in denial long enough. Phillip's declaration of love had eroded and demolished her arguments as swiftly as the incoming tide washed away a sandcastle. Sarah believed in a greater power, and her brush with death made her realize how fragile and precious life was. Phillip had experienced the same thing after being wounded on the battlefield. Who was she to throw away their love or to hold a grudge against the man who had wronged both her and Phillip?

Even the pain in her head diminished when he kissed her. The undeniable truth was that she loved him. He was not the only one who'd experienced love at first sight but refused to acknowledge it.

It occurred to her that the Black Widow of Whitehall had somehow managed to make this happen. The woman was prescient and observant, and must have discerned the mutual attraction between

Sarah and Phillip.

Another thought crossed her mind as she looked into his adoring eyes. Surely Alfred had planned this from the start. He'd placed her in the path of destiny. Tears filled her eyes. *You knew me better than I knew myself.*

"Sarah, my love, are you all right?"

Enfolded in his arms, her contentment was so great she had failed to answer his question. "What did you say, Phillip?"

"I asked whether you were all right." His face was etched with worry.

Silly—he probably thinks your memory is gone and damaged beyond repair. "No, what did you say before?"

"My darling, I said love is very precious and must never be ignored or cast aside."

"You are right. I've been a fool not to have seen it sooner. I love you, Phillip, and I don't want to live without you. But I can't help but wonder—do you think it possible Alfred planned this?"

Phillip's brow wrinkled as he contemplated her question. "Yes, I believe it's possible, from what I understand of him."

Sarah nodded, awed by her good fortune that the duke cared for her so wholly he'd seen to her future in every way, even providing a husband.

"Will you marry me, Sarah, and make me the happiest man in England?"

Sarah laid her hands on Phillip's broad chest. Their emotional interaction finally caught up with her, and tears of joy poured from her eyes. Her heart was so full of love that she could scarcely think. The turmoil had nearly eradicated her worst fear, her barrenness, but her love for him was so great that, taking a deep breath, she broached the subject. "Phillip, there is one other obstacle to our future, and I cannot in good conscious not reveal it to you. I fear I am barren."

His look of confusion gutted her. Was he having second thoughts upon hearing her confession? His reply was given in the gentlest of voices. "And you believe this because you never became pregnant with the duke?"

"Yes." Tears streamed down her cheeks, and she fought to catch her breath.

"Sarah, has it never occurred to you that the duke might no longer have been virile, and it was he that couldn't get you with child?"

Sarah's brushed away her tears. "And you are willing to take that chance?"

He chuckled, kissing the tip of her nose. "Not only am I willing to take that chance, but there is nothing that could persuade me to do otherwise. I love you, my darling, and God willing, you and I will have children. Marry me, Sarah. *Yes* is the only answer I will accept."

Happiness overwhelmed her. She wrapped her arms around him, hugging him tightly. "If you don't object, take me to Gretna Green. We can have a church wedding later. I never want to be apart from you again."

Chapter Eighteen

Gretna Green, Scotland
July 5, 1816

P HILLIP WOULD NOT leave Buckinghamshire, despite Sarah's insistence that she was well, until three days later, when the doctor confirmed she was safe to travel. They took the postal route at a leisurely pace in Phillip's carriage, and with resting the horses and overnight stays at inns along the way, they arrived eleven days later. The village of Gretna Green lay in the county of Dumfries and Galloway, just across the border between England and Scotland.

The village was notorious for its anvil weddings and hastily performed matrimonial ceremonies. It was the only recourse for lovers facing insurmountable marriage obstacles, such as being under twenty-one years of age and not having parental permission. Scotland, however, followed the Roman tradition of marriage being legal at the age of twelve for a girl and fourteen for a boy, with or without parental consent. Hence, Gretna Green was the only option for those struck by Cupid's arrow who wanted a legitimate marriage.

A church wedding would have been impossible regardless, as marriages between relatives, even if they were not of the same bloodline, were forbidden. They were commonplace enough but were recognized as void and voidable. Neither Sarah or Phillip expected any challenge to their union.

Phillip felt lightheaded, almost as if he were sleepwalking. He stood before the anvil priest and held Sarah's hands. His dreams were coming true, and his heart soared throughout the wedding service joining Sarah and him for the rest of their lives.

Even a grown man on the other side of youth can be nervous, he told himself, and he did his best not to tremble. Sarah, however, looked as calm and serene as an angel resting on a cloud. Her beauty was blinding, and he couldn't help but be reminded of the first moment he'd laid eyes on her walking toward him in the library at Waverly Castle. At the time, although he didn't realize it, her radiance captured his heart, and now she was his to love and to cherish for the rest of their lives.

Phillip's voice quivered as he repeated the ancient Celtic wedding vow. "Ye are blood of my blood and bone of my bone. I give ye my body, that we two might be one. I give ye my spirit, till our life shall be done."

Sarah's eyes filled with tears, and she squeezed his hands. In a feathery whisper of a voice that sent shivers through him, she repeated the vow.

In their haste to leave Buckinghamshire, all that could be procured were simple gold bands, which they slipped on each other's fingers. The sometime priest and sometime blacksmith pronounced them man and wife, and Phillip embraced his beloved Sarah and kissed her with all the love in his racing heart.

As experienced as Phillip was in the art of love, he was apprehensive. Everything should be just right for Sarah. His only thoughts were to please her in the marriage bed and awaken the woman of passion that he knew she was.

They dined on a light supper and finally settled into their room. A fire blazed in the hearth, and the innkeeper, in honor of their nuptials, had scattered red rose petals on the coverlet that perfumed the air.

Even with the efforts to create a romantic setting, though, when Phillip looked around at the spare furnishings, he wished this night, and all it represented, was unfolding at Waverly Castle.

He could not hide his dismay from Sarah, for she read his thoughts. "It's all right. We will rebuild and once again live at Waverly Castle. I pray our children will be born there."

"Of course you are right, but our first night as man and wife should be spent in pure luxury and indulgence. I want this to be memorable."

She went to him, placed her hands on his chest, and looked directly into his eyes. "And you think the setting will make a difference in the joy this brings us? Do you not see that our love is all that matters?"

She rolled her lips, moistening them. They glistened in the firelight, and Phillip could not tear his gaze away. A flash of lightning lit the room, followed by a deafening thunderclap, but it seemed muted compared to his pounding heart. His arms encircled her waist. "I swear to you, my darling, that I am not inexperienced, but when you are near me, I feel like a young lad unschooled in the art of love."

Sarah unbuttoned his shirt, and he stood as still as a soldier standing sentry. "If I could, I would erase every other woman you have ever loved from your mind. I am jealous of anyone who has ever held your affection." She giggled. "The only other man I have ever been with was Alfred, and ours was not a romantic union. But with you, my body comes alive, and I cannot control my desire to touch you." She opened his shirt and pulled it loose from his trousers. All the while, her eyes sparkled mischievously, watching him. She spread her hands on his bare chest, and he sucked in his breath. Heat and desire surged through his body, awakening his manhood. It was exquisite, and his confidence and passion mounted with every pulse, yet he still restrained himself.

For now, he was mesmerized by her taking the lead, for he had no doubt that at the right moment, control would be his. She had likely never experienced the ultimate bliss, the bliss he was determined to give her.

He whispered, "No need. I remember nothing of them. All I can see is you. All I will ever want, or need, is you. I love you, my darling."

Trusting he would not allow her to fall, Sarah leaned back, pulled the pins from her hair, and dropped them to the floor. Her red hair cascaded down her back, and he wanted desperately to run his fingers through her flaming tendrils. He firmed his hands around her waist, pulling her against him so she might feel what she'd done to him. He'd dreamed of this moment both asleep and awake so many times, but the reality of it made the blood in his veins race at a dizzying pace.

"Prove it to me, Phillip. Show me the depth and endurance of your love."

The erotic double entendre shot through him like a thunderbolt. Every muscle in his body grew taut with desire, unleashing the power of his passion. He clamped his mouth over hers, kissing Sarah with all the passion that had built up in his soul. The sweetness of her lips made him wonder how the rest of her would taste as his tongue danced with hers.

When they breathlessly broke apart, a fire was lit that could only be quenched by her. She pressed into him, sapphire-blue eyes open in a wanton look of hunger, making him want to charge forward and conquer the world for her. He held his horse back, wanting to survey her landscape before mounting his attack. But she was having none of it, and, stepping away from his arms, she began unbuttoning her blouse. His breath caught when her full breasts were finally revealed, tantalizing him beneath her shift.

Sarah breathlessly whispered, "I hope, Your Grace, you are not in any way disappointed?"

There was something unimaginably sexy about her using his formal address, given the intimacy of the situation. It was playful and teasing, and for the first time since he'd become a duke, it thrilled him to hear it from her just-kissed lips. He was filled with a protuberant power he couldn't disguise. The seam of his trousers was nearly bursting.

When she glanced down, it was so erotic that he could have spent himself without her even touching him. She leaned in seductively. "I believe my husband is a magnificent specimen of pure masculinity. I cannot wait to explore his attributes and discover what gives him pleasure."

"Be careful, my darling. You are playing with fire." Their sexy banter ignited visions of Sarah lying beneath him, her legs spread, begging him to claim her. His breath hitched as his attention became riveted on the slow unveiling of her full, round breasts that rose above her corset. Her dress slipped to the floor, and a shift, corset, garter, and stockings remained.

"Perhaps, Your Grace—or perhaps I like the thought of playing with fire. We've been hiding our feelings for so long that it's hard to contain my excitement."

"My darling Sarah, no words do justice to how I feel about you. Our wedding vows were a pledge, but this union of our bodies and hearts will bind us until death do us part."

"Phillip, may I remove the one thing that stands between us?"

"And what is that? Because I know of nothing that could possibly divide us."

With the gentlest touch, Sarah lifted Phillip's eye patch. He froze, fearing he would find repulsion on her face. Instead, she cupped the sides of his face, brought his face close to hers, and unabashedly kissed his eyelid. "My darling, your scar isn't at all off-putting, and when I think of your bravery, it fills my heart with the greatest admiration. I love every inch of you."

Relief filled him, and his love for her knew no limit. "You have not seen every inch of me yet." A husky chuckle rose from the deepest part of his chest.

"That is true. Something to be remedied posthaste. Perhaps you will help me remove my stockings? I really must lie down." She turned and bent over, picked up her dress, purposely giving him a most advantageous view of her perfect derriere. It aroused him enough that he pictured holding her hips and thrusting himself into her from that angle. By now, his virile member was aching to be put to work.

Phillip followed Sarah to the bed, and he watched her turn and sit with a bounce, which put her eye level with his bulging apparatus.

"The look on your face is priceless, my love," she teased. But her nervousness was betrayed by her trembling hands as she fumbled with the buttons on his trousers. When the last button was undone, she pulled his trousers and unmentionables down and curiously looked at his erect member. "Oh, my! I had no idea. I—"

"Dear Lord, Sarah, you married a much older man. Certainly you expected a difference." He smiled as his member hardened even more beneath her gaze.

She giggled and covered her mouth. "I don't think I knew what to expect, but seeing you, all of you, is profoundly stimulating."

"That works both ways, but talking about it will never come close to experiencing it," he said, pushing her gently back on the bed. He untied her stockings from the garters and slowly slipped each down her legs, then traced his tongue and lips down to her ankles. Her skin tasted of almonds and honey and had an erotic scent that could only be natural and exclusive to her. With each taste, each inhale, his cock grew more insistent, more eager to claim satisfaction. Seeing her closed eyes and the rapturous look on her face made it difficult to hold back and not mount her.

With great restraint, he rolled her over and undid the stays of her corset, kissing down her exposed back, all the way to her perfectly rounded buttocks. A soft, breathless moan escaped her, and she trembled as he rolled her back, tugged on the loosened corset, and flung it aside. Her eyes grew wide as he feasted on her naked beauty with his eyes. "You are so beautiful, Sarah." It pleased him that she didn't feign modesty and cover herself, allowing him a moment to admire her from head to toe.

Oh God, her breasts. He could spend hours on her breasts alone. He traced a finger along one dusky rose nipple and watched it pucker beneath his gaze, and then he did the same to the other. He couldn't resist the fluffy curls of red hair on her pussy, and he feathered his fingers over her, eliciting a most delightful moan.

"Oh, Phillip, I ache so desperately for you."

"Do you, my love? I will assuage that torment, but first…" He pressed his nose and lips to her curls and breathed her in before stretching her thicket open, kissing and sucking her delicate cleft of flesh.

Sarah's fingers found purchase in his hair as she trembled beneath his ardent tongue. She gasped with pleasure, her moans rising with each lap of his tongue. "Phillip, oh my… I never… Oh God!" Her hips rose and pressed against his mouth, and her hands gripped his hair as he licked and laved her secret nub of pleasure. And when he felt the spasms of her womanly core against his lips and heard her cry out his name as though in wonder, he knew he'd made her soar as she never had before.

SARAH HAD NEVER known such exquisite pleasure, such complete oneness with her own body. Every inch of her was in a state of arousal, and although she'd been loved before by the duke, never had she achieved that storied rapture that she'd read about.

Yet as perfect as her orgasm was from his lips and tongue, she hungered for more, and begging was not beyond her.

She needn't have worried—her stallion was as impassioned as she, and she was barely able to catch her breath before his mouth sought hers, and his tongue coaxed her lips open.

He massaged her breasts, tenderly teasing her nipples and caressing her skin until his hand found its way to her pleasure bud with the lightest of touches. Sarah could not contain herself, and gasped again, raising her hips to meet his fingers, as pleasure engulfed her once more.

Phillip's warm, ragged breath in her ear made her shiver with longing. "You are more sensual, my darling, than I ever dreamed."

"I cannot control my response—"

His finger slid inside and out of her steadily, stealing her words.

"So wet and inviting, my sweet." His lips claimed hers in another soul-stirring kiss as he positioned himself over her, slowly pushing his cock past her tender cleft of flesh, stretching her open. It was the most exquisite feeling she'd ever experienced.

He held himself inside her, and she felt him pulse and throb, every incredible inch of him stretching her completely.

"Please, Phillip," she said with a moan. "Make me yours."

With those words, a manly, guttural growl rumbled from his chest, and, with an urgency that matched her own, he began to move within her, thrusting in and out of her, faster and harder. She lifted her hips to meet every thrust of his magnificent member as he brought her again to the pinnacle of pleasure. She cried out his name over and over as she soared higher than she ever had before.

He continued to thrust inside her, and as he reached his own climax and shouted her name, she, incredibly, climaxed again. Their cries of love and fulfillment mingled together, and she knew she would never be the same again. Complete satisfaction was finally hers. She kneaded the muscles in his back as he rested inside her, whispering endearments in her ear, telling her how much he worshipped her. Sarah drifted on a sea of contentment, her lips pressed to his broad shoulder.

"Darling, you have given me your deepest self, and I am humbled." Phillip's lips lingered on her ear, his breath like a warm, tropical breeze that set her heart fluttering.

"Oh, Phillip, I never dreamed that love could be so all-consuming or so satisfying. You have awakened a fire in me that I fear will never be quenched."

"I should hope not." Phillip's chuckle rumbled from his chest. "I look forward to a lifetime of moments like this." He pressed his lips to her temple. "Let us take our rest before we begin again."

Sarah sighed. "Yes…" she whispered, snuggling closer into his embrace. She was grateful that the Black Widow of Whitehall had had the foresight to know whom she was meant for. Sarah couldn't wait to share her joy with Bess and thank her. Phillip was indeed the man of her dreams, and she knew she would always be blessed by the luck and love of the Lyon.

Epilogue

April 1, 1817
Buckinghamshire, England

Sarah pressed her lips to Luke Alfred Villiers' downy red hair. She was bursting with joy and snuggled into Phillip's embrace as he looked adoringly down on their newborn son. The dukedom's future was surely secured with Luke's birth, and today's christening was a celebration for the entire community. The townspeople filled the pews, their smiling faces mirroring those of the immediate family that were gathered around the baptismal fount at Christ's Church.

Sarah and Phillip had chosen the name Luke because it sounded like "luck," which was what they felt about their good fortune. Beside them, Lizzie and Lucien held their firstborn son, Grayson Radcliffe. The baby earl was also being celebrated with his christening, doubling the family's joy.

The bishop sprinkled holy water on each child's head and recited the prayer blessing them. Tears of joy slid down Sarah's cheeks, and Phillip bent and kissed them away. His lips found her ear, and he said, "Be happy, my love. This is the second-most splendid day of my life."

Sarah couldn't imagine anything more wonderful than today, but

Phillip was always full of surprises, including the magnificent white pearl necklace she was wearing that he'd given her on the day of Luke's birth. "And what is the first?"

"Why, the day I married you, of course." His brows knitted together. "It seems I may have been displaced by my son in what you consider your greatest life-changing event. I may have to work harder to keep myself in your good graces," he said with a chuckle.

She reached up and patted his cheek. "Never you fear, darling—you may be coming up short, but you are not far behind."

"Shush, you two lovebirds," said Agnes. "Honestly, must we all listen to your undying adoration of each other? Let the bishop finish or we'll never have our lunch at Waverly Castle, and I can only keep these children on good behavior for so long before all hell breaks loose." She covered her mouth. "Oh, dear me—forgive me, your excellency?"

The bishop roared with laughter. "I could not agree more, my dear Agnes. We are all"—he spread his arms wide, encompassing the packed pews of the church—"looking forward to the festivities. Our community is truly blessed." That brought a cheer from everyone in the church. The enthusiasm, however, furrowed the brow of the bishop, and he returned to his more serious countenance and proceeded with the christenings and blessed everyone in attendance. The multitude of godparents, including the veiled Bessie Dove-Lyon, looked on smiling.

Phillip, true to his word, had built a new and improved Waverly Castle, and the newly completed manor was even more beautiful than its predecessor. It was his gift to Sarah, and it replicated the turrets and architecture of Château de Chambord, a French Renaissance castle in the Loire Valley of France.

Sarah had found her happy-ever-after, and nothing on God's green earth could change that.

The End

About the Author

Belle Ami writes breathtaking international thrillers, compelling historical fiction, and riveting romantic suspense with a touch of sensual heat. A self-confessed news junkie, Belle loves to create cutting-edge stories, weaving world issues, espionage, fast-paced action, and of course, redemptive love. Belle's series and stand-alone novels include the following:

TIP OF THE SPEAR SERIES: A continuing, contemporary, international espionage, suspense-thriller series with romantic elements. TIP OF THE SPEAR includes the acclaimed *Escape, Vengeance, Ransom,* and *Exposed.*

OUT OF TIME SERIES: A continuing, time-travel, art-thriller series with romantic elements. OUT OF TIME INCLUDES includes the #1 Amazon bestsellers *The Girl Who Knew da Vinci* and *The Girl Who Loved Caravaggio,* and the new release, *The Girl Who Adored Rembrandt.*

THE BLUE COAT SAGA: A three-part serial, time-travel, suspense thriller with romantic elements set in the present-day and in World War II. THE BLUE COAT SAGA includes *The Rendezvous in Paris, The Lost Legacy of Time,* and *The Secret Book of Names.*

The Last Daughter is a compelling and heart-wrenching World War II historical fiction novel based on the life of Belle Ami's mother, Dina Frydman, and her incredible true story of surviving the Holocaust. The story begins at the dawn of World War II and follows the Nazi invasion and occupation of Poland, focusing on the Nazi's six-year reign of terror on the Jews of Poland, and the horrors of the death camps at Bergen-Belsen and Auschwitz, where more than six-million Jews along with other vulnerable innocents were slaughtered.

Belle is also the author of the romantic suspense series THE ONLY ONE, which includes *The One, The One & More,* and *One More Time is Not Enough.*

Recently, Belle was honored to be included in the RWA-LARA *Christmas Anthology Holiday Ever After,* featuring her short story, *The Christmas Encounter.*

A former Kathryn McBride scholar of Bryn Mawr College in Pennsylvania, Belle, is also thrilled to be a recipient of the RONE, RAVEN, Readers' Favorite Award, and the Book Excellence Award.

Belle's passions include hiking, boxing, skiing, cooking, travel, and of course, writing. She lives in Southern California with her husband, two children, a horse named Cindy Crawford, and her brilliant Chihuahua, Giorgio Armani.

Belle loves to hear from readers—
belle@belleamiauthor.com
Twitter: @BelleAmi5
Facebook: belleamiauthor
Instagram: belleamiauthor

Made in the USA
Monee, IL
07 December 2023

48457193R00095